IN HOT WATER...

Clint fell back into what little of the water was left. Both of his arms were draped over the sides of the tub as a thought suddenly popped into his head. "You know what we need right now?" he asked.

"What?"

"Some more hot water."

She started to laugh, but stopped when she saw the way Clint's expression suddenly turned very serious. "What's the matter?" she asked.

Sitting perfectly still, Clint whispered, "Listen."

The slow, subtle sound that they heard wasn't Mario's snoring. It was a creak in the floorboard, someone approaching their room. That sound was followed by the groan of hinges as the narrow door suddenly burst inward...

THE GUNSMITH

265

LONG WAY DOWN

J. R. ROBERTS

J
JOVE BOOKS, NEW YORK

LONG WAY DOWN

A Jove Book / published by arrangement with
the author

PRINTING HISTORY
Jove edition / January 2004

For information address: The Berkley Publishing Group,
a division of Penguin Group (USA) Inc.
375 Hudson Street, New York, New York 10014.

ISBN: 0-515-13660-3

A JOVE BOOK®
Jove Books are published by The Berkley Publishing Group,
a division of Penguin Group (USA) Inc.,
375 Hudson Street, New York, New York 10014.
JOVE and the "J" design
are trademarks belonging to Penguin Group (USA) Inc.

PRINTED IN THE UNITED STATES OF AMERICA

10 9 8 7 6 5 4 3 2 1

ONE

"Clint Adams! Am I glad to see you."

In a way, it would have been funny for Clint to think about just how many people gave a wide smile before delivering bad news. Truth be told, he couldn't easily count how many times he'd been suckered in by a friendly face or a few kind words which lasted just long enough for him to let his guard down like a dimwitted boxer.

Although he didn't like to let himself become too pessimistic, Clint still had a reflexive twitch in the back of his head when folks seemed overly glad to see him. There were a few exceptions, of course, but unfortunately Manuel Ortiz wasn't one of them.

Instead of letting his arrival in Los Rios Verdes be spoiled right off the bat, Clint put himself in a more positive frame of mind. Of course, there was still that part of him that was bracing for the short, stinging jab.

"How's it going, Manuel?" Clint asked, shaking the hand offered by the smiling Mexican.

Manuel was lean and muscular, with a narrow face and slightly sunken cheeks. His skin was naturally dark, but also had the appearance of smooth leather that had been left out to soak up the sun for years. Roughly Clint's height, Manuel had broad shoulders and moved with a natural strength and grace. His eyes were dark and alert, reflecting the beaming smile that covered the lower half of his face.

"I could complain, but who'd want to hear it?" Manuel replied with a wink. "How long have you been in town?"

"Not long. I rode in last night."

"And you didn't come to see me?"

"I didn't see much of anything," Clint said. "Apart from the inside of my hotel. I've been on the trail for a week and just about passed out the minute I set myself down on that bed."

Leaning in a little closer, Manuel nudged him and said, "I'll bet you weren't alone in that bed, eh?"

"You'd lose that bet."

"*Qué es esto?* Clint, my friend, it sounds like you're getting old. The man I knew wouldn't have had any trouble getting one of these lovely ladies to lay beside him."

"Then maybe I'm getting old and tired."

Manuel made a sound that was part exhale and part laugh. "Don't talk that way, because that only means I'm getting older, too."

"Well, it sure beats the alternative."

Laughing wholeheartedly, Manuel slapped Clint on the back and started walking toward the nearest building. He'd been standing outside savoring a thin, cheap cigar when he'd spotted Clint, and now he turned to point himself back toward a door that was propped open by an empty clay jug. "You have a good way of looking at things, my friend. Now let's get you out of the sun so I can buy you a drink."

"Sounds like a good idea."

Los Rios Verdes was one of those towns that wasn't much more than a glorified train depot with two rows of buildings stretching out in either direction from the station. There were all the basic amenities, but the place still managed to feel deserted. That could have been because not one of the buildings was more than a few years old. But as Clint had gotten up and taken a morning stroll to work some of the kinks from his legs, he realized that all but a few of the buildings were businesses of some kind. It almost felt as though the town's entire population came and went by rail.

Manuel strutted toward the building marked "The Rum Runner" as though he owned the place. He kicked open the front door and made a straight line for the bar, which still smelled of freshly split lumber. "A beer for me and my friend here," he said to the bald old man behind the bar. Turning to Clint, he added, "My treat."

"Much obliged," Clint said. It was a little early to be drinking, but Clint knew better than to refuse the offer, since there probably wouldn't be another one for some time.

While the bartender took his time in cleaning out a pair of mugs and filling them with the brew, Manuel leaned one elbow upon the wooden surface and asked, "So what brings you to California? Last I heard, you were causing trouble farther east."

"Actually, I was helping out some folks who lost their sheriff about a month ago in a town a few days' ride north from here. They got a replacement, but that man wouldn't take the job unless he had someone reliable to finish up what he'd been working on."

"Let me guess. That someone was you, right?"

Clint shrugged. "It's really not much of a job. Just delivering documents to a judge in Sacramento. You ask me, I'd say the man who was doing the job before only took it because he was getting paid by the day and nobody seemed to be in too much of a hurry to see it done."

Manuel grinned and nodded. "Some people are like that. Still, it sounds like a good job. There's nothing better than working for someone with deep pockets."

"I wouldn't know. All I get out of the deal is the sheriff staying where he's needed rather than riding around soaking up someone else's money. Well, that plus my own expenses."

"You could get some more, I'm sure. Or even come up with some expenses to make it worth your while."

Clint ignored that suggestion and sipped the beer he was given. "So what's been keeping you busy? Last time I saw you, you were riding shotgun for Wells Fargo shipments."

"Not enough money in that line of work."

"I thought you were in it for the thrills and adventure. You know, fighting off robbers and Indians and such."

"Did I ever really talk like that?" Manuel asked with an embarrassed flinch.

"You sure did. And don't go back to saying we're older now, because that doesn't cut it with me."

"All right, then. But you can't exactly make me sound like a wide-eyed kid when you're the one who'd rather be homeless and on the trail just for the sake of rooting out some excitement of your own."

"Point taken. So what have you been into lately?"

Manuel puffed his chest out proudly and raised his mug as if he was about to toast his own good fortune. "I'm in business for myself, amigo. A man can only take orders for so long before he has to strike out on his own."

"Congratulations. What kind of business are you in?"

"Actually, that's what I wanted to talk to you about."

Aw hell, Clint thought, trying not to flinch. *Here comes the jab.*

TWO

It didn't matter how many drinks Manuel bought him, Clint couldn't help feeling as though he'd be paying for them one way or another. When he got that feeling, that payment was never made in something so easy to come by as money.

Since he'd been watching Clint's face fairly closely, Manuel picked up on the subtle shift in his expression. "What's the matter, amigo? You look like you're not so happy for me anymore."

"Go on," Clint said, taking a deeper pull from his beer. "I'm listening."

Satisfied enough to put his mind at ease for the moment, Manuel fixed his eyes on Clint and lowered his voice even though there were only a handful of other people in the saloon. "I'm a tracker, Clint. A tracker of fugitives from the law."

"You mean a bounty hunter?"

"Yes. It's more excitement than I've ever had. Hunting down the most dangerous animal in the—"

Clint let out a sharp laugh that cut Manuel off in mid-sentence. "Jesus, Manuel, the way you sell it you'd think you'd read too many yellow-back novels."

5

"That's some talk coming from someone whose name shows up in those books more often than I can count."

Not wanting to go near that particular subject, Clint let it drop and just took another sip of beer.

"As I was saying," Manuel continued. "I'm in business for myself and have actually been doing quite well. In fact, I was thinking about hiring some outside help for this newest job of mine, and here you show up like a gift from above."

Clint rolled his eyes, but didn't say anything to break Manuel's stride.

The more the Mexican talked, the more excited he became. He did manage to keep his voice down, but just barely. That was a moot point, however, since nobody else in the place seemed the least bit interested in the conversation.

"Did you hear about the robbery of the Wells Fargo train that was headed for San Francisco?" Manuel asked.

After thinking for a moment, Clint said, "No."

"Really? It was in the newspapers."

"I didn't hear about it, Manuel. Just go on with the story."

Although he couldn't hide his disappointment in the fact that his fame wasn't as far-reaching as he'd thought, Manuel forced himself to move on anyhow. "It was a very big robbery. Very messy."

"How messy?" Clint asked, already fearing what the answer would be.

"They got away with twenty-seven thousand dollars and killed eight men along the way."

"Guards?"

"Mostly, but there were a few others that got in the way. Passengers or a conductor or something like that," Manuel said with a vaguely dismissive wave of his hand. "The law is out for blood and Wells Fargo is right behind them. Between the two, there's a fifteen-thousand-dollar reward for all three of the men who did this. The leader alone is worth six."

Whistling softly, Clint said, "That's a hell of a reward considering how much was taken. But it's usually not strictly a matter of money in things like this."

"You can say that again. The law wants to hang them for the murders, and the Wells Fargo men want to show that it's never a good idea to steal from them."

"So it sounds like business is good for you," Clint pointed out. "Where do I fit in?"

"You, my friend, fit in where my old partner used to be. He was killed not long after I decided to go after these animals. That leaves me short-handed, and I don't think I can do this job with the help I have left."

"In case you don't remember, I'm not a bounty hunter, Manuel."

"I know, I know. But a man has to earn a living, doesn't he? And you always were fond of lending a hand to the law." Manuel turned so that both elbows could be propped on top of the bar. Shrugging, he said, "Maybe I thought you'd be interested in seeing these killers brought to a judge, especially since you were on your way to a judge anyway. But if you'd rather make your delivery, I can always find someone else."

Clint shook his head, grinning at the shameless way the Mexican was trying to play upon his emotions. "Spare me the guilt. I'm immune."

"Then what about doing a favor for an old friend?"

"It sounds like you've got things well under control, Manuel. I know plenty of men in your line of work and I doubt you'll have any trouble finding someone to take your partner's place. Besides, running this package to Sacramento may not be an adventure, but it's a job I said I'd do, and I'm not about to just push it aside."

Manuel took one last swig of beer and nodded. "All right, all right. I know that tone of voice, just like I know how bullheaded you can be. At least do me a favor and think about my offer."

"I'll do that."

"Good enough. Now, don't tell me you need to get back on the trail right after this drink, or I'll know you're trying to get away from me."

"No, I'm taking a train into Sacramento, which doesn't leave until tomorrow."

"Excellent. Then we can still catch up on old times and see what kind of trouble we can start in this place. What do you say to that?"

"I say it sounds pretty good to me. Just don't try to buy all my drinks, or I'll know you're bribing me into signing on to this new business of yours."

Holding up his hands as though he was on the wrong end of a robber's pistol, Manuel said, "You got me, amigo. Since I won't be able to bribe you, the next round is on you. But don't worry," he added with a smirk. "I'll get my partner to chip in, too."

"Partner?"

Manuel nodded. "*Sí.* Connover's a good worker, but not the kind who can handle everything I need for a job like this." Pointing toward the back of the room, the Mexican added, "Take a look for yourself."

Just then, Clint heard someone stepping up behind him. The footsteps seemed especially loud since the floorboards were every bit as new as the rest of the saloon. The wood rattled beneath Clint's feet, announcing the other person's presence. Clint wasn't surprised until he turned around to take a look at who the new arrival was.

Clint felt a hand set down upon his shoulder. Unlike Manuel's grip, this newer one was more subtle but still carried a strength of its own. The fingers resting upon Clint's shoulder traced along the base of his neck as the other person walked over to stand between the two men.

What caught Clint's eye was the face of the person stepping up to the bar.

Her face was pale, but only in comparison to the thick, dark brown hair that framed it. Standing next to Manuel made her look even more distinctive, because she was the same height as the Mexican and shoved him aside as though he was a troublesome sibling. She had high cheekbones and full lips which curled up at the edges into a friendly smile.

"I'm Susan Connover," she said, extending her hand rather than waiting to be introduced by Manuel.

"Clint Adams."

She appeared to be impressed, but only let it show in her eyes. "Manny says you'll be working with us. I'm really looking forward to it."

Still shaking Susan's hand, Clint shot his eyes over to Manuel, who'd already made sure to be looking in another direction entirely.

THREE

Clint thought it was funny the way Susan didn't seem to have any trouble at all believing that Manuel was stretching the truth. All Clint had to say was that he hadn't agreed to taking any job just yet, and she shrugged and swatted the Mexican with a quick backhand.

"Actually," she said to Clint, "I was surprised you were really here at all. If I believed everything that came out of Manuel's mouth, I would think he knew everyone from Wild Bill to General Lee and that he had a part in putting down Billy the Kid himself."

Manuel straightened up and said, "Hey, I did meet Wild Bill."

"Sure you did," Clint chimed in, even though he knew that Manuel was actually telling the truth on that one. "And I bet you even beat him at cards, too."

"I did! You were there!"

Clint managed to keep a straight face for another second or two before he busted out laughing. "If you don't make it as a bounty hunter, you can always try your hand as a salesman."

"I've been telling him that for weeks," Susan said.

After a few halfhearted attempts to salvage some of his

dignity, Manuel bought another round of drinks and all three of them lined up at the bar to finish them off. Talk quickly turned to swapping stories and comparing scars, with Clint playing his tales down while Manuel made himself sound like the second coming.

Clint noticed that Susan didn't add any stories of her own to the conversation, but it was hard to say whether that was because she didn't want to talk or because she simply couldn't get a word in edgewise. Before Manuel could launch himself into another of his exaggerated yarns, Clint looked to the attractive woman and smiled.

"So what made you want to throw in with a dog like this?" he asked, motioning toward Manuel with his mug.

Susan smirked and replied, "He pays well and doesn't hold out on me. Besides, I know he's full of shit most of the time so I just think of his stories as a way to pass the time in between jobs."

"What?" Manuel said, pretending that he was bent out of shape by her words. "You told me you never had so much excitement as when you were riding with me."

"Did I?" Susan remarked. "Then I guess you're not the only one that's full of shit."

Lifting his mug in another toast, Clint looked to Susan and said, "Now, that's the way to keep a bullshitter in line. My hat's off to you."

Susan returned the smile, letting her eyes linger on him for a bit longer than what would be considered just friendly. "Just your hat? We'll see about that, Clint Adams."

Manuel let out a grumbling laugh while shaking his head. "Look out, amigo. She's *muy peligrosa* when she sets her sights on someone. Very dangerous."

"You speaking from experience, Manuel?" Clint asked.

Before the Mexican could answer the question, Susan cut in by saying, "He wishes." She shifted on her feet, inching a little closer to Clint while brushing her leg against his.

Until now, Clint hadn't been able to see much of Susan's body that wasn't covered by her battered trail clothes, which didn't look much different from the things Manuel was wearing. Both of them had dusty shirts with the sleeves rolled up to their elbows and pants that might have been dragged from behind a horse for a day or two.

That, however, was where the similarities ended. Over the last half hour or so, Susan hadn't bothered to straighten her shirt as it shifted on her body. All but the top two buttons were secured, but as she'd been moving and gesturing, the somewhat baggy shirt had worked its way down until Clint could see a bit of her generous cleavage.

Her skin was dusty as well and somehow she made that work to her advantage. There was just enough dust on her skin to make her look rugged and unashamed to get down and dirty if necessary. For a moment, as he glanced down at the curve of her breasts, Clint imagined cleaning her off with a wet towel, taking his time to explore her body fully.

She had a few spots of dust on her face as well, which Clint hadn't noticed until she'd gotten a little closer to him. Now that she was close enough for him to notice such things, Susan gave him a different kind of smile that said she didn't mind letting Clint soak in the sight of her.

"So what do you think?" Clint asked her in a softer tone of voice. "Should I be careful of you?"

Reaching up with one hand, Susan kept her eyes squarely on Clint as she tugged at one of the buttons of her shirt that remained open. For a second, it seemed as though she was going to peel the shirt off a bit more. Instead she pulled it down just enough to give Clint a peek at the softer, paler skin below that button and then fastened it to cover herself up all the way.

"You're going to have to make up your own mind," she said. "And I guarantee you won't rest until you do."

With that, she let her hand drop to her side and stretched out her fingers until they brushed against Clint's thigh. Susan moved her own leg up onto the rail beneath the bar, covering up the fact that she was letting her hand stay on Clint's thigh and moving it up farther between his legs.

Already feeling a stirring within himself, Clint fought to keep his hands off her when he felt her fingers brush against his growing erection. He knew she was the type of woman to do what she pleased, but her forward move just then surprised even him. Letting out a breath as she slid her hand away from him, Clint moved his eyes back up until he was looking at Susan's pretty, dusty face. "You're right about that. Somehow I get the feeling I won't be doing much resting at all while I'm in town."

"That doesn't sound like a bad thing."

"It isn't. I just wish I had more time to wait and see what comes up."

The heat in Susan's little grin was unmistakable as she said, "And who says you have to wait?"

FOUR

After a few more intense moments passed, Manuel leaned forward so he could be better noticed by Clint and Susan. "I see the two of you are getting along, so that means we can talk about business for a minute? I mean, I hate to interrupt you if you'd rather just sit and stare at—"

"That's fine, Manuel," Susan said after peeling her eyes away from Clint. "Talk all you want."

It took Clint a moment to get his mind back onto anything else but the feel of Susan's hand between his legs or the curve of her body beneath her baggy clothes. Not that he was completely captivated by the brown-haired beauty, but she was much more appealing in his mind than talk of any business.

Reluctantly, Clint looked toward the Mexican and said, "You want me to leave so you can talk business with your partner here?"

"Uh, no. Not at all. The business has to do with you. Or at least it can if you accept my proposal."

"I already told you, Manuel. I've got business of my own in Sacramento."

"And I can help you with it, amigo. I've been around

14

here long enough to hear some things you might find interesting."

Clint studied the Mexican's face for a moment and shook his head. "And here I thought we were friends. You'd hold out on telling me something important just to get me to do something for you?"

"No. Not at all."

"Then what you heard isn't very important?"

"I didn't say that. But I, uh . . ."

At that point, Susan concentrated at a spot on the bar directly in front of her. She hadn't really found anything interesting to look at, but she was trying to keep herself from laughing at the way Clint was getting Manuel to squirm in his boots.

It wasn't long before Manuel saw what Clint was doing also. Instead of laughing, however, he spun on his heels until he could press his back against the bar. "Ah, to hell with both of you," he said with an aggravated wave toward Clint and Susan.

"Sorry, Manuel," Clint said. "It's just that you make it so easy for me to give you a hard time. Go on with what you wanted to say."

Manuel sulked for another solid couple of seconds before turning to look at Clint once again. "You forgot to ask me something, amigo."

"Really? What's that?"

"You forgot to ask me how I knew you were coming to Los Rios Verdes."

Clint took a moment to think back to when he'd first entered town and when he'd first met up with Manuel. Although it hadn't been more than an hour ago, Clint felt as though he'd missed something by the way the Mexican eagerly awaited a response to the question he'd posed. Finally, Clint just had to shrug and ask, "You knew I was coming to town?"

"*Sí.*"

Knowing he had to play into whatever dramatics Manuel was trying to build, Clint said, "All right then. How did you know I was coming to town?"

"I'm glad you asked. There were some men waiting around the train station for the last couple of days. Rough types, you know? I thought they might be trying to get the drop on me, so I had Connover keep an eye on them."

Before Clint said a word to her, Susan looked over to him. "They never even heard of Manuel."

"*Sí.* Lucky for them. Not so lucky for you, amigo. They were waiting for you because they thought you'd be on a train passing through here and wanted to make sure you didn't get to your destination."

"How do you know all of this?"

Manuel grinned. "My new partner is very persuasive. She has a way about her. Perhaps you've noticed?"

Clint was actually proud of himself that he managed to not react at all when he felt Susan's touch quickly press between his legs. "Yeah," he said evenly. "I've noticed."

"Then you won't be surprised to know that she got these men to say quite a bit to her. Part of what they said was that they were waiting for a famous man to come through this town and that they meant to make sure he only left it feet first."

Turning to Susan, Clint asked, "Who were they?"

She shrugged. "I don't know. They gave me some names, but it wasn't anything that would do anyone any good."

"Try me."

"Dusty and Wade," Susan replied. "That's what the two I talked to called themselves. They weren't about to give me any last names."

"Do those names mean anything to you?" Manuel asked.

Clint thought for a moment, but didn't have to take long

before shaking his head. "Not especially. What else did they say?"

Leaning against the bar, Susan took her beer in both hands. "Just that they meant to kill some well-known man. All it took was a few kind words and some wide eyes before they told me they were gunning for you, Clint. They figured I would be impressed after they dropped your name."

"Were you?" Clint asked.

"Not a bit. That's mostly because I figured they were lying just to get on my good side or maybe to get into my pants." Shooting a glance over toward Manuel, she added, "They wouldn't have been the first to try something like that."

She didn't seem too bent out of shape when she said it. When Clint followed her gaze over to Manuel, he got an embarrassed smile and a shrug from the Mexican. After all, a man should never be faulted for trying his luck.

"Could these men have anything to do with this job of yours?" Manuel asked, quickly steering the conversation back onto a favorable track.

Clint considered it for a moment. "Could be."

"What exactly are you carrying to Sacramento, amigo?"

"That's business, Manuel. My business."

Knowing when to back off, the Mexican let the subject drop and quickly headed into cooler waters. "I guess it doesn't really matter why they're after you. It does matter that they're out for blood. Connover didn't have to tell me that for me to figure they were men to be reckoned with. A man in my line of work knows how to tell when a gun is being worn for show or when its owner is serious. That, my friend, is my business."

Clint nodded and took Manuel's words at face value. The Mexican might have been fond of blowing smoke sometimes, but any bounty hunter worth his salt had to be able to size up a threat from a blowhard. Clint knew the other man well enough to trust his assessments in that area. If Manuel didn't know enough to make those kind of judgments, he would have been dead already.

"You said these men are at the train station?" Clint asked.

"*Sí*. They've either been waiting there or at the little cantina next to the platform."

"And there's two of them?"

"Three," Susan corrected. "Maybe more. I only talked to two of them, but there was at least one other man, who didn't take his eyes off the trains long enough to give me a glance."

Clint finished off his beer and wiped the foam from his upper lip with the back of his hand. "I appreciate the warning."

"You going to pay them a visit, amigo?"

"Not just yet. My train doesn't leave until tomorrow. They can wait until then to see me. If they can't wait that long, let them come to me."

FIVE

Clint put a little extra bravado into his voice when he said that last part and even wore a smug grin when he spoke. Although Susan seemed to like the sound of it, he put on the display for someone else's benefit.

As he played up the moment with some help from Manuel, Clint kept watch on a solitary figure out of the corner of his eye. He watched a man who was standing alone at the farthest end of the bar. That man had been nursing the same drink for some time and had looked away quickly when Clint glanced in his direction earlier.

When Manuel had been talking about recognizing a potential threat, the Mexican's words had sparked something in the back of Clint's mind. It was at that moment that Clint took extra notice of the gun worn by that solitary figure, along with the cold, predatory gleam in that one's eyes.

Rather than call attention to his possible discovery, Clint began sending out signals just to see if they would be received. Not only were they received, but Clint even managed to catch a few signals coming from the other man as well. Apart from the way the figure snapped his head toward Clint's end of the bar, there was also a smug, self-satisfied grin that appeared on his face.

Surely the man didn't think anyone had paid him the slightest bit of attention. And now, after listening to the way Clint had carried on, he was probably thinking of the best way to make Clint eat his own words. To the other man's benefit, he didn't let too much slip before turning his attention back to his own drink and ignoring everyone else completely.

Clint indulged in some more casual banter with Manuel and Susan as he waited for another sign of movement coming from the spot he was still watching at the outer edge of his field of vision. The solitary figure gave it another half hour or so before he decided he'd heard enough. Waiting for some of the other locals to get up from their table, the man fell into step behind them and headed for the front door.

Just as the other man walked by, Clint leaned in closer to Susan and whispered, "Don't make a big deal out of it, but take a look at that fella walking out right now."

Susan didn't acknowledge Clint's request with a word or even a nod. Instead, she glanced toward the front of the saloon as though she was merely stretching her neck. Her eyes didn't stay in one spot for more than a fraction of a second until she turned back around and looked down at her drink.

"That's one of them," she said. Her voice was a bit louder than a whisper, but the man had already left the saloon and closed the door behind him.

"Are you sure?" Clint asked.

She nodded, glancing around the rest of the saloon. "He was the one I didn't actually talk to, but I saw him with the others long enough to know he's one of them. That's the third one I was telling you about before."

"He was watching us."

"*Qué?*" Manuel interrupted. Leaning in so he could hear more of what Clint and Susan were saying, he added the strong smell of beer and bad breath to the air.

"Not so loud," Clint said. "You need to lay off the beer for a while."

"Why, amigo? You worried that Tom might have heard too much of what we were saying?"

Clint and Susan both turned to look at the Mexican square in the face.

"Tom?" Susan said. "Who's Tom?"

"That one that was over there," Manuel answered, hooking a thumb toward the farthest end of the bar. "He just left."

"And why didn't you mention him before?" Clint asked, trying his hardest to keep his patience. "Didn't you think it was important?"

"Oh *sí*, it was important. I just thought Susan had already seen him since he was sitting there most of the time we've been here. What did you want me to do? Walk over and point him out to you when he thought he was being so clever and spying on us?" Manuel tapped his temple with his forefinger and winked. "Better to let him think he has the upper hand. I've learned to take advantage of that in this new business of mine."

As much as Clint thought he should be angry with the Mexican, he couldn't deny that Manuel had a good point. It would have been nice to have heard something earlier, but that very well could have tipped their hand.

"Now that he's gone, is there anything else you'd like to tell us?" Clint asked.

Manuel scrunched his eyes shut as though the process of thinking was actually starting to physically hurt him. He then shook his head and let out a laugh that he'd been trying to suppress. "You should see the look on your face, amigo. If I didn't know better, I'd say you wanted to take a swing at me. I was just waiting for Tom to leave."

"Well, the good news is that these guys still think we don't know much about them or that I know where they are," Clint said. "The bad news is that they might be getting a little bold right about now. Especially since they know where to find me."

"So where do we go from here?" Susan asked.

Manuel jumped on that question as though he'd been waiting with baited breath for anyone to ask it. "We can trick them into making their move and then turn the tables on them. That way, we can be done with that mess before we go to bed tonight, and we can move on from there fresh tomorrow morning."

"Tell you what," Clint said. "If you want to run straight into a fight, then you go right ahead, Manuel. So far, these guys haven't made a real move against me yet. I could still use some rest and some real food to help soak up some of this beer we've been drinking."

"So you'd risk them ambushing you?"

"The sad part is that I'm used to people ambushing me. Mentioning my name around too many men who fancy themselves to be gunslingers is like lighting a fuse. Until the explosion comes, I plan on relaxing for a bit. And you," Clint said, offering his arm to Susan, "are coming with me."

Susan was smiling broadly when she wrapped her arm around Clint's and followed him out of the saloon. Manuel watched them leave before leaning both elbows back onto the bar and ordering another beer.

SIX

As Clint and Susan walked out of the Rum Runner, the population of Los Rios Verdes seemed to double right before their eyes. The source of the surge of population was easy enough to see since a large passenger train sat steaming on the platform, hissing like a giant beast. As people streamed from within the iron shell, some of them merely stretched their legs upon the platform, while even more headed for the row of buildings.

The sun had dipped below the horizon and the train station was a little ways from the saloon, so Clint couldn't see much by way of details in that area. He glanced over there to see if he might be able to spot the men that were supposedly waiting for him there, but only found a large, milling crowd.

"You want to go over there and take a look?" Susan asked, following Clint's line of sight. She did a pretty good job of glazing it over, but the disappointment could still be heard in her voice.

Clint shook his head once and didn't change the direction he'd been walking. "Nah. If they're so willing to wait there for me, they won't be going anywhere anytime soon."

"And if they've decided to stop waiting?"

"Then we won't have to go to them." As he spoke, Clint put on a confident smile, which spread quickly onto Susan's face.

"This really doesn't bother you, does it?" she asked.

"I don't mean to brag, but I really have had people gunning for me before."

Hearing that put an excited gleam in Susan's eye that was plain to see even in the quickly approaching night. Not only did Clint spot the gleam, but he knew he'd put it there when he'd given her that last reassurance.

If there was one thing that drew women to him, it was confidence. That wasn't a trick specific to Clint by any means, but it was still something in short supply with most folks going about their daily lives. There were some women who also got a thrill from hearing talk about fights in the street and dangerous living.

Those were definitely things that Clint knew plenty about, and he'd recognized Susan as one of those thrill-seekers from the moment they were introduced. Then again, she would have to have that as part of her personality if she was going to work so closely with a bounty hunter and troublemaker like Manuel Ortiz.

"So how long have you two been in Los Rios Verdes?" Clint asked.

"Long enough to know a good place to eat and where the softest beds are in town."

"Now, that's what I call being one step ahead of the game."

She smirked and shrugged. "I'd like to say that I had a knack for scouting out anything and everything within two days, but it takes less than half of that time to see all there is to see in this place."

"I'll bet Manuel wouldn't have any trouble finding some way to make himself look like a genius for knowing the same things."

"Yeah, I'll bet you're right. So you two go pretty far back?"

"We go back a ways," Clint admitted. "Far enough for me not to buy into much of what he says until I check up on it myself. Manuel's heart is in the right place, but he's just a . . . well . . ."

"A bullshitter."

"Ah, you seem to know him pretty well yourself." After she'd come to a stop along the side of the street, Clint looked up at the building where Susan had led him.

They'd walked up to one of the smaller structures on the side of town farthest from the train station. Even so, the sound of the steam engine still moved through the air like a living thing, threaded with the jumble of all the passengers talking among themselves. The new arrivals made it about halfway down the street before they either found someplace that caught their interest or lost the energy to walk any farther.

A few of the passengers looked down the street at the spot where Clint and Susan were standing, but turned their backs on them once they got a look at the building the couple had chosen. Once Clint's eyes became more adjusted to the thickening shadows, he could see the details better for himself. The building was squat and had no second floor. Like all the others in town, it smelled of fresh lumber, as well as something else that tickled Clint's nose.

"This looks like a bathhouse," he said. "Smells like one, too."

"You have a good eye and a better nose."

"Are you trying to tell me that I need to wash up before we do anything else tonight?"

Laughing a bit, Susan walked up to the narrow front door and pulled the handle. "Not unless you want to. Actually, this place is run by an Italian family who serves food at a few tables in the back of the place. Hardly anyone knows about it, and they practically give the food away. Not only that, but there's no way for anyone to sneak in and listen to us like they did in the saloon."

Either he knew what to smell for this time around or his stomach was putting ideas in his head, because the next breath Clint took was laced with the hint of fresh bread and oregano. "You managed to track down good food and a safe spot all at once? I think Manuel shouldn't be the boss out of you two."

"Well, then I'd have to listen to his bragging even more, if he knew he had to compete with me."

"If that food is half as good as it smells, there's no competition. Besides," Clint said as he slid both hands over her hips and pulled her in a little closer to him, "you've got some nice eyes, yourself. And skin. And lips."

With that, Clint leaned in and kissed her. Their lips touched for a moment, each person enjoying the feel of the other before pressing in for more intense contact. Susan tasted like fresh air and her skin felt smooth and inviting. Clint couldn't help but wonder what the rest of her body felt like as he breathed in her pure, natural scent.

"Come on," she whispered. "We should get inside before anyone spots us."

"You're the boss."

SEVEN

Even though he figured Susan had her facts straight, Clint still felt a bit foolish wanting to eat dinner when he went into a room filled with bathtubs and partitions. The bathhouse was a small, open space just big enough to fit three tubs sectioned off by folding wooden panels for privacy. At the back of the room, there was another row of smaller doors lined up like storage spaces.

Sure enough, the man who greeted them had olive skin and thick black hair framing a face lined with deep creases. One of the back doors came open a crack, allowing a woman with the same Italian features to peek out into the main room.

"Fifty cents for a bath and all the hot water you need," the man said in a thick Italian accent. "For an extra ten cents, you can even have one of the private rooms with the scented salts."

"Hello, Mario," Susan said, stepping up in front of Clint.

The older man squinted and grabbed the closest lantern so he could thrust it forward to illuminate the two of them. Once he got a better look at Susan's face, he smiled and nodded. "Ah, back again, eh? You bring a friend this time." He said that last part in a tone that sounded like a suspicious father sizing up the company his daughter kept.

"I sure did. I was hoping Carmella might be able to cook us some dinner."

Still eyeing Clint with open suspicion, Mario said, "He just come in on this train? You should be more careful with the strange men that want to say nice things just so they can—"

"Hush, Mario," the woman in the back room interrupted. She pushed the door open and came through, wiping her hands on a blue and white checked apron that was tied around a more than generous waist. The woman had the shape of an apple and a face with enough life in it that she could have been anywhere from forty to sixty years old.

Carmella swatted her husband's arm as she walked past him, smiling warmly at Susan and even more warmly at Clint. "Forgive the old man, please. He still thinks all women are too weak to look out for themselves. You want to eat? I cook for you."

"That's great," Clint said. "It smells wonderful."

"Oh, that's just some bread I make for tomorrow," Carmella said with a quick wave. "I cook real dinner for you two kids. Please come in and have some wine."

Since Carmella seemed more than happy to fuss over him and Susan, Clint was more than happy to let her. The Italian woman showed them into the back room from which she'd come, which turned out to be a cramped kitchen with two little round tables just big enough to seat a pair of diners at each.

Susan was right when she said the spot was a perfect place to eat and relax. Not only did the food make Clint's mouth water, but it came quicker than he could have ever hoped. Throughout their meal, the front door only opened twice, and Clint could hear everything as plain as day through the back door, which Carmella kept cracked open as she worked.

Just as if he was inside a small home, Clint didn't even have to strain his ears to hear who the few other people were who'd come into the place or what they said as they did their business and left. The only way for someone to sneak up on them in that building was if someone found a way to move without their feet touching the floor. Even if that was the case, Mario made enough noise to wake the dead.

Carmella made a dinner of Italian sausages served piping hot on a bed of pasta. That, along with the bread that Clint had smelled when they'd arrived, was enough to fill his belly and tickle every taste bud he had. Not only was the meal cheap, but Carmella even seemed uncomfortable taking any money for it at all.

"*Grazie,*" she said once Clint finally got her to accept payment.

"And don't forget this," Susan added, handing over another couple of coins. "As long as we're here, my friend might as well clean up."

Carmella looked a little unsure as she held the additional payment in her open hand. "We are going to close before you get here."

"Well, never mind then," Clint said, feeling a little embarrassed at her reaction as well as the fact that someone else was willing to pay for him to bathe. "I can come back tomorrow morning when you—"

"No, no," Carmella said suddenly. "You are a good girl and a nice man. I know I can trust that you will behave. Mario will wait out front and lock up after you leave."

The old man was on his feet and gave his wife a peck on the cheek. Once Carmella left the place, Mario turned and shuffled over to another of the small doors at the back of the room.

"Take your time and don't worry about me," he said to

Clint as he opened the door next to where they'd had their meal. "I have a good book to keep me company. Just let me know if you need anything."

Now that he looked in at the tub, Clint found the prospect of a hot bath rather appealing. Already, his bones were aching and the trail dust felt like an unwelcome second skin that he couldn't wait to remove.

The private room had a small stove that already had a pot of water boiling on top of it. There was some cooler water already in the tub, and once the two were mixed, it made for a perfect pace to soak a weary body after a long day.

Clint's ears were still listening for any trace of someone else trying to get the drop on him, but that didn't stop him from savoring each moment as he shed his clothes and lowered himself into the soothing water. There were plenty of jars of salts with different scents, but Clint just grabbed some soap and balanced it on the edge of the tub for later.

Clint sank down into the water and rested his head against the back of the tub. The large basin was old and had been worn enough so that the inside was particularly smooth against his shoulders. He lost track of the minutes as he let himself unwind, but was suddenly snapped back into full awareness when he heard someone approaching the door to his room.

Straining his ears even further, he realized that he could no longer hear the familiar sounds of Susan's or Mario's voices. In fact, he couldn't hear much of anything except for the footsteps that carefully drew closer and eventually stopped somewhere on the other side of the door.

Knowing that whatever sounds he made could be heard just as easily through the door, Clint moved slowly until he was sitting upright in the water. His eyes remained focused on the door as his hand reached out for the pile of his clothes and the modified Colt waiting underneath it.

The handle twitched and the door swung slowly inward just as Clint's fingers wrapped around the Colt's handle. Before he lifted the pistol to aim for the door, he caught sight of a face peeking in on him.

EIGHT

Clint let out the breath he'd been holding and set the Colt down. "Jesus, Susan, that's a good way to get yourself hurt."

She stepped into the little room and slowly shut the door behind her. "Didn't mean to startle you."

"Did Mario leave?"

"No. He's sleeping."

"And what about what Carmella said? You know, about her being able to trust us?"

Susan's smile was made up of equal parts humor and trouble as she approached the tub and slowly pulled open the buttons on her shirt. "I guess she made a bad call on that one, because I'm not a good girl. Actually," she said as she peeled off her pants and let them drop to the floor, "I'm a very bad girl indeed."

Clint sank back down into the water and watched as Susan let her hands wander over the front of her body. Her shirt was completely unbuttoned and hung off her shoulders. She let her hair fall forward as she slipped her hands up underneath the bottom of the shirt, hooked her thumbs through the side of her panties and peeled them off as well. When she straightened up again, she slid both hands through her long brown hair and stretched her back luxuriously.

Clint felt a hunger growing from deep inside of him as he watched her sensuous display. The sides of Susan's breasts could be seen through the gaping opening in her shirt and the nipples became erect as they brushed up against the coarse fabric.

As she stepped into the water, Susan used both hands to slide the shirt off and let it drop onto the floor behind the tub. Her breasts were pert and firm and her body was accentuated by tight muscles that writhed beneath her skin. She kept her eyes locked on him the entire time as she lowered herself into the water and moved forward until she was straddling Clint's waist.

"I hope Mario is a sound sleeper," Clint said.

Susan smiled, slid her hands beneath the water and stroked Clint's penis in slow, steady strokes. "Why do you say that?" she asked. "Do you plan on making a lot of noise?"

"Not necessarily. But you might." Without giving her a chance to say another word, Clint reached under the water and slipped both hands around her waist. From there, he pulled her forward until the tip of his cock brushed against the smooth lips of her vagina.

Susan's eyes went wide with surprise at the sudden move and she fought back the urge to let out a little moan. Knowing what he was trying to do, she shook her head and waved her finger as though she was scolding a schoolboy.

"Naughty, naughty," she teased.

"And here I thought you'd like that sort of thing."

Tightening her legs around him, she swiveled her hips back and forth, rubbing her pussy against his hard shaft. "Well, you thought right." She maneuvered herself until the tip of his cock was perfectly positioned and then bit her bottom lip when Clint thrust into her.

NINE

Susan gripped both sides of the tub and squatted over him so she could move up and down directly on top of him. "We'll have to keep quiet," she said while riding Clint's rigid column of flesh. "We might be in trouble if we're caught like this."

Clint moved his hands over her body, cupping her breasts, which were just big enough to fill his grip. "One thing's for sure, that would certainly blow our cover as a nice, respectable couple."

"I honestly wasn't trying too hard to keep that up. All I wanted was an opportunity to get you alone."

"Well, you've got it," Clint said as he slid both hands around to grasp her buttocks. "Let's take full advantage of it."

Using his muscles as well as the water itself to lift her, Clint positioned himself so that Susan was leaning against the other end of the tub and he was between her legs. He kept his hands on her backside so he could hold her up and pull her toward him when he pumped inside of her with strong thrusts.

Susan's body glistened with moisture and her hair was slick against her scalp. The motion of both of their bodies caused the water to slosh around them like a miniature storm, which was like a gentle massage against their naked skin. Thrusting into her one time harder than the rest, Clint grabbed her buttocks tightly and drove his cock deeply within her warm body.

Pressing her head back against the tub and arching her back as the powerful sensation rushed through her, Susan almost let out a cry that would have most definitely brought some unwanted attention. At the last second, she held it back and the groan remained inside, sounding more like a growl.

When she opened her eyes, she glared at Clint as though she was going to scold him for what he'd done. But it was obvious that the act of holding back the screams she so desperately wanted to voice made every other feeling that much more intense.

Clint could feel her excitement in the way her body clenched around him and her nails dug into his shoulders and back. He felt her nails drag against his chest and then was surprised a bit himself when she pushed him back and away from her.

She seemed to genuinely enjoy the expression on Clint's face, because Susan smiled broadly as she dug her heels into the small of Clint's back to keep him from going too far back. Then, after reaching behind her to grab onto the tub where her head was resting, she thrust her hips forward and back in an almost serpentine motion.

Clint was still inside of her when she began moving that way and almost made a few sounds of his own when Susan slid him in and out of her by shifting her lower body in that fashion. Pulling him in closer by using her legs, she clenched her muscles until her pussy was tight around him and then slowly eased herself back again.

He had to take a few deep breaths as he moved back against his end of the tub. The pouting expression Susan wore when he was no longer inside of her was strangely attractive and disappeared the moment he brushed the tips of his fingers against her clitoris.

"Remember," Clint whispered before putting a finger to his lips and letting out a slow "shhhh."

Susan glanced quickly over to the door as though she'd completely forgotten about Mario, and the rest of the world for that matter. They both got quiet and stayed that way just long enough to make sure there were no noises coming from the main room.

When he heard a rumbling snore seeping through the door, Clint took hold of Susan by the waist, pulled her forward and moved her body as though he was going to flip her onto her stomach.

Susan reacted instinctively to where Clint was leading her and moved so that she had her back to him and was facing her end of the tub. Once again grabbing hold of the sides with both hands, she slid her legs on either side of him and backed up until she felt him bump against her.

Taking a moment to admire the sight before him, Clint looked down at the delicious curve of Susan's back. Her spine arched in anticipation, and the muscles in her shoulders flexed. He rubbed his hands over the small of her back and then along the wet skin of her buttocks.

Most of the water had either evaporated or gone over the side by this time. The level stopped short of Susan's waist as she knelt in the tub and leaned her chest against the side. She closed her eyes and waited to feel Clint move behind her, purring softly when his hands brushed along her hips and he positioned himself between her legs.

He reached between her thighs and massaged her moist vagina for a few moments before slipping his cock into her from behind. As he slowly pushed all the way inside of her, he watched as Susan's entire body tensed and she tossed her head back while flipping her hair over her shoulders. Since it was long enough to reach his hands anyway, Clint took hold of her hair and pulled just enough to take up the slack.

Susan moaned softly when she felt the resistance keeping her head from moving, pushing herself back against him to make his thrusts pound against her even harder. Every time she felt him slam against her, Susan struggled to keep her passionate cries from escaping her lips. To make up for the noises she couldn't make, Susan gripped the side of the tub even harder, until her knuckles turned white with the effort.

Clint pumped into her again and again, making the water churn around him as his hips slammed against her tight buttocks. Every time his cock slid inside of her, Clint could feel Susan tightening and releasing. Her breathing seemed to fill the room, since that and the moving water were the only sounds to be heard.

He could even hear her orgasm approaching as her breathing became faster and faster as his thrusts quickened to match the pace. His own climax overtook him quickly, coursing through him as Susan arched her back even more and reached behind her to get her hands on any part of Clint she could reach.

He leaned forward so she could touch him with her grasping fingertips. The moment her hands found the sides of his face, they slid into his hair as far as they could. Clint quickly moved his palms over her sides until he could reach around and cup both of her breasts. Her nipples were hard and wet, and she trembled a little when he pressed them between his thumb and forefinger.

Her body shook with the sensations that raged through her flesh, making Clint's own orgasm even more intense. He exploded inside of her until he thought he didn't have enough strength left to support his own weight. Susan felt the same way and nearly dropped onto the side of the tub once she let out the deep breath that had built up within her body.

Turning around to face him as she exhaled, Susan shook as the last tickles of her climax worked their way through her system. Finally, she leaned back against the side of the tub, closed her eyes and let a satisfied smile creep over her face.

Clint also fell back into what little of the water was left. Both of his arms were draped over the sides of the tub as a thought suddenly popped into his head. "You know what we need right now?" he asked.

"What?"

"Some more hot water."

She started to laugh, but stopped when she saw the way Clint's expression suddenly turned very serious. "What's the matter?" she asked.

Sitting perfectly still, Clint whispered, "Listen."

The slow, subtle sound that they heard wasn't Mario's snoring. It was a creak in the floorboard, someone approaching their room. That sound was followed by the groan of hinges as the narrow door suddenly burst inward.

TEN

The door hadn't even slammed against the wall before a pair of men came charging into the room with their guns drawn. Two more men were right behind them. All four of them were wearing scarves wrapped around their faces that came up to just above their noses, leaving only their eyes to be seen peering out from beneath their hats.

The first man into the room walked right up to the bathtub and stuck the barrel of his gun in Clint's face. "Don't move, asshole," he snarled.

"You too, honey," the second one said, aiming his pistol at Susan, who'd also been about to jump out of the tub to get to her clothes.

Clint didn't have to see much of the second man's face for him to tell that he was staring at Susan's naked body. Although a little awkward, Clint was glad for any kind of distraction he could get in a situation like that. He figured he could apologize to Susan once it was over.

"What the hell is this about?" Clint asked, letting his anger burn through like a fire that raged behind his eyes. "If you're looking to rob us, then you're out of luck. Our money's back at the hotel."

By this time, the other two men had taken up their

positions in the room. One stood at the head of the tub, between Clint and the first man. The fourth stayed in the doorway, keeping tabs on everyone else inside the room as well as glancing back to look in the main room behind him.

It was obvious that the first man had noticed Susan's wet, naked body, but he wasn't allowing himself to be distracted by her. The other three men weren't quite as disciplined, however, and kept letting their eyes wander over to her shapely figure.

Proving that she truly did belong in this dangerous business, Susan let the men ogle her all they wanted. In fact, she didn't even lift her arms to cover herself since that would have only let the other three men focus their thoughts onto something else.

Good girl, Clint thought.

"You know damn well we ain't here to rob you, Adams," the first man said. "We are here to claim something that belongs to us, and if you know what's good for you, you'll hand it over right now." He punctuated his last word by extending his gun hand a little farther and pulling back the pistol's hammer with his thumb.

The metallic click rattled through the room menacingly but didn't bring out the slightest reaction from either of the gunman's targets.

"All right then," Clint said, keeping his eyes level with those of the lead gunman. "Are you going to tell me what exactly you're after or do I have to guess?"

"We want the only thing you got that's worth a damn thing. Them papers you're bringing to Sacramento."

"And why would you want that? They're just some documents for a judge to sign."

The third gunman had been getting anxious, and he stepped forward to snarl almost directly into Clint's ear. "Yeah and once he signs 'em our lives ain't worth shit! You know that."

"Well, I know it now, don't I?"

There was a moment of tense silence, but it didn't have much to do with Clint or Susan. The lead gunman was staring daggers into the one who'd just spoken, until the third man stepped back and gave the rest of them some breathing room. "Dusty, keep your goddamned mouth shut."

Clint twisted around until he could stare at the head gunman fully in the face as he said, "Wade Hanssen? Is that you under there?"

The lead gunman used his free hand to pull the scarf down away from his nose and mouth. "You're the real detective, aren't you, Adams? And here I thought you were just a delivery boy for the law that was too cheap to pay for their mail to be shipped regular."

"I never claimed to be a detective," Clint said calmly, as if the gun in his face wasn't even there. "I actually didn't even care what those documents were."

"So you won't have any trouble handing them over."

"Well, there's where you're wrong. I'm supposed to deliver those papers and that's what I'm going to do."

"Not if you don't live through the next minute or two, you won't."

Glancing around at each of the four men in turn, Clint said, "So these are warrants for you men?"

"Federal warrants," snarled the third man, who still wore his scarf.

"All right. Federal warrants. You think that just by intercepting them here all your legal troubles will go away?"

"We ain't stupid," Wade said. "We just need some time to finish up some business. Collect some old debts, things like that, before we head for the border."

The second gunman still had his eyes glued to Susan's breasts and was breathing heavier by the second. "And we got some bastards we need to visit. Ain't that right, Wade?"

"That's right. The local law ain't much of a problem, but we can't do much with the federals on our tails. So what have you got to lose, Adams? Hand over them papers, we'll leave you and your whore here, and you can deliver the next warrants that get written up."

"And by that time you'll be long gone?" Susan asked.

Wade didn't take his eyes off of Clint for a second when he replied, "That's the idea."

"And once you get what you want, you'll just let me and the girl go?" Clint asked. "Is that what I'm supposed to think?"

"That's what I'm tellin' you."

In the time since the men had stormed into the room, Clint had been moving his hand closer and closer to the Colt stashed under his clothes. He wasn't close enough to draw the weapon yet, but he'd managed to gain a precious inch or two while the gunmen had either been looking at his face or Susan's body.

"How about if I tell you that I don't think your word is worth spit?" Clint said.

Wade's grin was more like the one worn by a skull. Shrugging slightly, he stepped back just enough to move his face away from Clint. "It don't matter none anyway. Once you're dead, we can take all night to find them papers. Then we'll take our time with your lady here."

ELEVEN

Clint steeled himself in preparation to make his move. He knew he would probably take a bullet or two. The only thing he could do was try to stay alive. He looked over to Susan just to make sure that she was preparing herself as well. There were no signals passed between them. None were necessary.

She was ready. Clint could tell that much by the grim determination in her eyes when she glanced back at him.

The rest of the gunmen prepared themselves to follow Wade's lead. For the first time since their arrival, the second masked man took his eyes away from Susan's exposed body. That lasted just long enough for him to get confirmation from his leader, and then he licked his chops and aimed his gun at her. His eyes darted straight to her skin, which had air dried in front of him, and he pulled the scarf from his face to reveal a wide, gap-toothed smile.

Clint recognized the cold look in Wade's eyes as the calm before the storm. That would last for another second or two as he wrapped his mind around taking the life of another human being. Once that passed, his eyes would clear up, as though they'd died a little on their own. That was the moment Clint was waiting for, and until it came,

43

time itself seemed to drag by on leaden feet.

Trying to draw out the moment for as long as possible without forcing Wade's hand, Clint stretched his arm a bit more since it was behind the tub and out of the lead gunman's sight. Dusty might have seen, but he was too busy preparing himself to fire as well and didn't notice where Clint was reaching on the floor.

Clint's fingertips touched his shirt and pushed through until he hit the leather of his gun belt. Although it was only a matter of less than an inch, it might as well have been a mile between himself and his Colt. He shifted in the tub as if he was starting to get uncomfortable, which gave him a little more distance to reach.

At that moment, Wade's eyes started to deaden. His mouth became a straight line and his finger tightened around his trigger.

The man standing in the doorway took a step forward, shuffling his feet on the clean floorboards. "Psst," he whispered. "Wade, you got to see this."

Without turning away from Clint, Wade snarled, "What the fuc—"

He was cut off by a shot that thundered through the little room like an explosion. The shot came from the doorway, hissed through the air and drilled a hole into the back of Wade's skull. Blood sprayed out of a larger hole as the bullet blasted out of Wade's head, coloring the warm bathwater with droplets of crimson.

For a split second, everyone in the room was stunned. Clint was surprised just as much as the rest, but managed to pull himself together faster than anyone else. Although he didn't know exactly what was going on just yet, Clint leaned over the edge of the tub and pulled his Colt from where it had been laying the entire time.

The moment the gun was in his grasp, Clint felt complete once again. By the time he turned around to aim at the nearest gunman, he saw that Susan had sprung to her

feet in the tub and was making a grab for the pistol held
by the man who'd been leering at her since he'd arrived.

Her left hand closed around the middle of that man's
gun so she could push it up to point at the ceiling while
she smashed her right fist into his jaw. Her knuckles im-
pacted with a wet slap and a crunch. The blow she'd
landed was powerful enough to loosen the man's grip on
his weapon, so she could then take it away from him and
toss it into her right hand.

The gunman closest to the one in the doorway spun
around to take a shot at the man who'd killed Wade. They
fired simultaneously at each other, filling that part of the
room with a cloud of thick smoke. But Wade's killer
looked to still be breathing.

Since Susan seemed to have her end under control for
the moment, Clint swiveled to get a look at the gunman
now closest to him. Dusty's eyes were wide with surprise,
but he'd had the presence of mind to keep his gun aimed
at his original target.

Clint had his eyes focused as well and let his body go
through its motions as he kept close watch on every move
Dusty was making. The gunman was covered in Wade's
blood, but he was still shaking himself out of his shock
rather quickly.

Knowing that he had to fend for himself, Dusty began
pulling his trigger even before he got his mind completely
settled from the initial shock. Less than two seconds had
passed since the first shot had been fired, but already it
seemed like a lifetime ago.

And if Clint didn't play his cards right, that lifetime
was about to come to an abrupt end.

TWELVE

As he brought the Colt up to fire, Clint let his body twist onto its side and drop down into the tub. In a fair fight, he wouldn't have had a bit of trouble with the likes of these men. But because he'd had a gun in his face since before he'd been able to arm himself, Clint knew this was anything but a fair fight.

Dusty pulled his trigger, but he was still aiming at the spot where Clint had been rather than where he'd put himself in the meantime. The gun bucked in his hand and its bullet took a chunk out of the side of the bathtub, which allowed some water to spill onto the floor.

Feeling the hot lead pass by his rib cage, Clint squeezed his own trigger and sent a round through the air. He knew more than just one round would be needed since the awkward motion of his twisting dive would surely pull his aim off by an inch or two.

That shot didn't hit its mark, but it came close enough to send Dusty away from the tub using hurried, shuffling steps. Clint couldn't have asked for more from that hurried shot he'd taken, and he used the second or two that he'd bought himself to give himself a steadier position within the tub.

Just as he'd gotten his legs beneath him into a tight crouch, Clint heard another wave of shots rip through the air. Two of the shots came from the doorway. Another came from the man Susan was wrestling, and the last came from Dusty, who'd managed to aim and pull his trigger in record time.

Clint heard the wood crack apart as he felt the bullet shred through the meat in his left leg. Blood immediately spewed from the wound, clouding the water so he couldn't see the extent of his injury. He couldn't tell from how the leg felt either, since the salted water felt like a hacksaw being dragged across its entire length.

Every one of Clint's senses felt as though they'd been sent to their breaking point. Rather than let the pain get the better of him, Clint gritted his teeth through it and clasped his Colt in both hands to keep the gun steady.

As the tub emptied through all the fresh holes that had been blown into its sides, Clint dropped back until he felt his shoulders touch the bottom and had both feet pressed against the end. The Colt's barrel was just above the water line as he sighted down its length and aimed through the hole that Dusty had just shot through the wood.

Clint couldn't see much through that hole, but he could see that something was blocking the light from getting in the way it should. Since Dusty's crouching form was the most likely thing to be blocking that light, Clint let out a steadying breath and squeezed his trigger.

The Colt let out a thunderous bark and spat out a tongue of smoke and flame. But the bullet didn't leave much in its wake, since Clint managed to send it straight through the existing hole and into what was on the other side.

Hollering in pain, Dusty straightened up and clutched at the fresh wound in his gut. Even through his winces and cries of pain, he had the gun almost leveled at Clint's face when the Colt was fired again.

Clint hadn't adjusted his aim by much, but it was

enough to focus in on a target that he could clearly see. That target was the center of Dusty's face, and he put his bullet through the gunman's eye half a second before Dusty pulled his trigger.

The gun in Dusty's hand went off, but that was only because every muscle in his body twitched as the last bit of life sped out of him. His good eye was just as wide as the gaping hole in the second socket as he froze for a moment and then dropped onto the floor like a sack of rocks.

Susan was still struggling with the man whose jaw she'd dislocated with a single punch. Mangled obscenities sprayed from his mouth, along with streams of bloodied spittle, as the gunman tried to reclaim his weapon. He had one hand closed over Susan's and used the other to push her arm up to keep the weapon pointed at the ceiling.

So far, the gun had gone off a few times, but Clint couldn't be sure whether or not there were any bullets left to be fired. At that moment, Clint saw that there had been another gunman in the mix that he didn't even know about until that very second.

He'd thought there were four, the only ones he could see. But since Dusty and Wade were dead, there should have been only two left, including the one who'd started the whole scuffle by taking a shot at Wade to begin with. Susan still had her hands full with her man, and the one near the doorway was still struggling with someone as well.

Clint chalked up his miscalculation to stress under fire and left it there. Whatever the reason might have been, it didn't matter since there was still a situation he had to wrap up before he could think for too long about much of anything.

The gunman struggling with Susan was beginning to press his arm down, despite one hell of a fight coming from her end. Strained breath hissed out of his mouth like steam once he knew he'd gotten over on his opponent. The gunman began twisting his wrist to point the pistol's barrel at Susan's face.

Knowing he had precious little time to act, Clint shouted, "Susan!"

That was enough to catch her attention and draw her eyes over toward him. The moment she saw what Clint was doing, she lowered her head and hunkered down as far as she could without taking her hands away from the other man's wrist.

He didn't have a completely clear line of fire, but Clint did have a clean enough view of where he wanted his bullet to go. Adjusting his aim with a subtle tilt of his wrist, Clint squeezed his trigger and sent his first bullet through the other man's elbow, digging a messy channel through muscle and bone.

With her attacker's gun arm rendered all but useless, Susan had no trouble at all pulling the weapon completely from his grip once again and dropping down into the tub.

Another shot roared over her head, slamming into the gunman's chest and dropping him straight back onto the floor. Getting up with the gun in her hand ready to fire, Susan looked at Clint and then over to the two men struggling in the doorway.

"Should we just let them go at it?" she asked.

Clint shook his head. "We owe one of those men a favor. Time to pay up."

THIRTEEN

Already sighting down the barrel of his Colt, Clint stood perfectly still and watched as the two men threw each other back and forth. For the moment, the one who'd fired the first shot had his back to him and was blocking most of the man he was fighting. Clint only had to wait another couple of seconds before they took hold of one another and slammed against the door frame.

Squeezing his trigger the moment he had a shot, Clint put a bullet into the nearest man's leg, taking all the wind from his sails and dropping him to the floor like a stone.

As the thunder of that last gunshot echoed through the little room, Clint shifted his aim so he could point the gun toward the last of the masked men still standing. That one still had his arm cocked back next to his ear as though he was ready to deliver a punch. His eyes were wide and darting back and forth over the scarf that covered his face.

"Take it easy, mister," Clint said. "You've earned yourself some time to explain yourself, but not enough to make a fool out of me. Start talking and drop the gun."

"I'm out of bullets," came a muffled voice from behind the scarf.

"Drop the gun anyway."

The man complied, but still didn't raise his hands right away. "Put the gun down, Clint, for Christ's sake."

At that point, Susan started to walk forward, but suddenly remembered that she wasn't wearing a stitch of clothing. "Is that . . . ?" she asked, quickly grabbing for the clothes piled up on the floor near the tub. "Oh my lord! It is!"

Clint could tell that the man with the scarf was smiling just by looking at his eyes. He tensed when he saw that man reach out toward Susan, but that was just a reflex. The rest of his mind already knew he had nothing to worry about from that one, since he'd finally heard enough of the voice to recognize it through that scarf.

"Manuel," Clint said with a relieved sigh. "What the hell are you doing?"

The Mexican had been reaching for Susan's shirt, which was closer to him than it was to her. He tossed it over to her and pulled the scarf away from his face. "I'm saving your ass, amigo. Couldn't you tell?"

Instinctively, Clint lowered his Colt, as though he was going to drop it into its holster, and squirmed the moment he realized he wasn't wearing the holster. Not only that, but he wasn't even wearing his pants. But it looked like that bullet had only scraped him a bit. He hopped out of the tub, stepped over the bodies laying nearby and dug into the pile of his clothes.

Manuel squatted down beside the man who was still writhing on the floor and grabbing the wound that Clint had put in his leg. Using the barrel of his gun, the Mexican pulled down the other man's scarf, revealing a scowling, pitted face. "John Rogan," he announced. "You're not worth as much as the rest, but at least you're alive. For the moment, anyway."

In less than a minute, both Clint and Susan had their clothes on and buttoned enough to cover the most important parts. After buckling on his gun belt, Clint went over

to each of the masked men in turn and collected their guns
before making his way over to the doorway. Clint didn't
recognize the name John Rogan, but he must have been
a wanted man since Manuel was leering down at him as
though he was made of gold.

"Are these the men you were telling me about?" Clint
asked. "The ones that were waiting at the train station?"

Standing back up, Manuel nodded and said, "*Sí*. These
are the ones, all right. But they won't be going to any
more stations for a while, eh?" When he said that, Manuel
pressed the toe of his boot against John's leg wound until
Rogan was squirming on the floor like a worm.

"Knock it off, Manuel," Clint ordered after taking
John's gun. "Help him to a doctor."

"Why? He will only swing once he gets where he needs
to go, anyway."

Hearing that, Rogan stared up at the Mexican. The pain
in his leg suddenly didn't seem to bother him as much as
listening to what Manuel was saying.

Manuel played up to the ember of fear he saw in the
gunman's eyes and nodded slowly. "Oh, you'll hang, señor. No doubt about that."

"Then I'll hang," Rogan shot back. "At least I won't
have to listen to you anymore."

"Talk tough now," Manuel said evenly. "But when you
get that rope around your neck, you'll be a different man.
You'll be standing up on those gallows looking out at
everyone watching, and you'll see that it's a long way
down from that platform to the end of that rope. I hear
that it feels like you're falling forever just to get to the
end."

"That's enough, Manuel," Clint said.

The Mexican stopped talking, but knew his point had
already been made. He could see that by the fear that had
grown in Rogan's eyes no matter how much the other man
tried to suppress it.

Handing over one of the guns to Susan, Clint asked her, "Do you think you can watch Mr. Rogan while I have a word with our personal savior here?"

Susan nodded, took the gun and checked to see how many rounds were still in the cylinder. "No problem. He doesn't look like he's got much fight in him anyways."

Clint walked past Rogan and Manuel without giving either man much of a glance. He didn't have to, since both of them did just what they were supposed to do without needing any further direction. Manuel followed Clint into the main room and Rogan stayed right where he was, staring uncomfortably down the barrel of the gun in Susan's hand.

"That was a close one, amigo," Manuel said as he pushed the narrow door shut.

"That much I know already," Clint said while looking around the room. "Now how about you fill in the parts I don't know?"

FOURTEEN

"I'll even save you some breath," Clint said as he walked toward the front of the main room. "You can start with the old man that should have been sitting at that desk right over there. Did you see him when you and the rest came in here?"

Manuel furrowed his brow and looked as though he was a second away from scratching his head when he finally brightened up and nodded. "Oh, *sí*! I remember the old man. He almost got himself killed quicker than you did. Wade came in first and was about to have that old man's throat cut just to keep him from making noise."

Clint's heart jumped, and he rushed over to the desk where Mario had been sitting.

"But I came in and knocked him out instead," Manuel continued. "He'll have a headache, but at least he'll wake up, no?"

Clint was kneeling behind the desk, crouching over Mario's quiet form. He was worried at first when he spotted dried blood on the old man's scalp, but he quickly saw that Mario was breathing steadily, as though he was in a deep sleep.

"He will wake up, won't he?" Manuel asked with a bit of worry tainting his voice.

"He'll wake up, Manuel."

"Oh, *muy bien*."

"Yeah. That is very good." Clint slid a towel under Mario's head that had been laying on the floor behind the desk. From there, he straightened up and turned to face the Mexican. When he thrust his hand out, Clint noticed that Mario flinched a bit before grinning and shaking it.

"I thought you looked angry, amigo."

"The blood's still pumping pretty fast, but it's slowing down a bit. I'm grateful for what you did in here."

"*Es nada.* After you and Susan took off on your own, I got tired of sitting around the Rum Runner, so I did some work of my own. I went to the station because there was a train pulling in, and with all the people coming and going, I thought I could get closer without being noticed."

"You went looking for Wade?"

Manuel nodded. "Found him, too. Him and two others who were all gathered together like they were a firing line or something. They must have thought you were headed to that train for sure, because they were ready for a fight.

"I did get up closer to them and saw them get even more itchy when you didn't arrive. They started talking loud enough for me to catch most of it, and they decided they'd waited at the station long enough. That's when the fifth man showed up, and he said he'd seen you come here with some woman."

"So there was five of them?" Clint asked.

"That's how many I saw. Wade told three of them to follow him so the fifth could cover their backs. After the first four left, I followed the fifth and waited until he was by himself. He was so wrapped up in what he was doing that I got right in behind him and knocked him out before he knew I was there. After that, all I had to do was take some of his clothes, get over here and wait for my chance. You know the rest."

"And where's the one you took out before getting here?"

"Stuffed behind some crates a little ways down the street."

"Any chance he could be awake yet?"

Manuel thought about that for a second and shook his head. "Not unless he's got steel in his head. I wasn't nearly as careful with him as I was with the old man over there. Even if there are more of them around, I doubt they'll be anxious to do anything once they realize Wade and these other three won't be coming back."

"That was some quick thinking, Manuel. Thanks again."

The Mexican shrugged and replied, "It's all a part of this business, amigo. That's why it should only be left to men like us."

When he noticed that Mario was starting to stir, Clint felt his nerves settle a little more. "What about the old man's wife? Did you see her when you came in here?"

"No, but I think I should be able to narrow down where to find her. It's a small town, after all."

"That it is. I guess we should get back in the next room to take that asshole off Susan's hands."

Manuel smirked. "I know her for a long time. I'd bet money she's doing just fine and that it's him that's hoping we come back to take her away from him."

Just to be sure, Clint peeked into the next room and saw Susan jamming the barrel of her gun into the other man's face and speaking to him in a quick, angry whisper. Clint couldn't quite make out what she was saying, but whatever it was, it had turned the gunman white as a sheet.

"Then again, I think you're right," Clint said, stepping

back and shutting the door so he wouldn't be noticed. "She's doing just fine."

Manuel held out his open hand, motioning with his fingers for Clint to hand over the bet he'd just won.

"I owe you a drink," Clint conceded. "How's that?"

"Good enough for me."

Clint shook his head and dropped himself down onto the stool that Mario had been using when he was conscious. "Dammit, how could I be so stupid? I knew they'd be coming sooner or later and they still managed to get this close."

Manuel stepped forward and put his hand on Clint's shoulder. "Don't feel too bad, amigo. A man like you always has someone coming for him, and you can't live your life looking over your shoulder. That's not even living."

"Maybe not, but it would keep me from almost getting shot in a bathhouse."

Although he tried holding it back, Manuel was unable to hide the smile that came onto his face. That smile quickly turned into a laugh when he said, "Don't be so hard on yourself, amigo. Sometimes the best man gets caught with his pants down."

FIFTEEN

When Clint and Manuel stepped back into the smaller room, the last remaining gunman looked as though he'd just been sprung from the bottom of a dungeon. There was actually some gratitude in his eyes when Manuel walked over to Susan and gave her a hug, taking her away from where she'd been looming over the gunman.

"That bitch is crazy," the gunman said.

Clint looked over the fallen man and noticed that there was some ripped material cinched around the wound on his leg. "Maybe, but I see that she patched you up so you didn't bleed to death."

His eyes darting between Clint and Susan, he said, "She said that was just so I would be around long enough for her to . . ." He seemed to let the sentence taper off simply because he didn't want to think about the rest of it himself. "That bitch is crazy," he said with considerably less steam than the first time.

Clint walked up close and put his toe against the gunman's wound with just enough pressure to let the man know he was there. Although he wasn't the sort to torture a man while he was down, there was no reason for the gunman to know that.

"Call her a bitch again," Clint said calmly, "and you'll wish you were in the same place as your friends over there."

Hearing that made the gunman's eyes flick over to the bodies, which were still laying on the floor throughout the room. It was plain to see that he'd been trying to ignore those open, clouded, dead men's eyes, but being in the same room with them was having an effect on him all the same. Of course, that was exactly why Clint had left him in that room to stew for a bit in the first place.

"What's your name? John Rogan?" Clint asked.

The gunman let out a breath and stared up at Clint. He tried to put on a tough expression, but couldn't quite mask the fact that he was glad to be looking at someone else besides Susan or his dead partners. "That's right, but what the hell do you care?"

"And how many are in your group here in town, John?"

"There's more of us. You'd better believe that."

"I sure hope you're not talking about the man that was wearing this, *cabron*," Manuel said, tugging on the scarf and coat he still wore. "Because he's not much better off than you right now." Turning a meaningful gaze over to the corpses, he added, "Or them."

"The rest of us," Rogan said slowly, "they probably left by now. You'll see them soon enough."

He was lying. Clint had played poker with far better liars than this one and was able to read the signs written all over the gunman's face. Then again, Rogan also didn't seem to have the steam left to pull off a lie good enough to fool anyone at the moment. But Clint let him have his dignity and decided not to call the gunman's bluff just yet.

"I probably will see them," Clint said. "And when I do, you can bet they won't get half as close as you did to-night."

The room was silent except for Rogan's haggard

breathing. Even though Clint had moved his foot away
from his leg wound some time ago, the gunman still
squirmed as though something was pressing down on top
of him.

"All right," Clint said after studying Rogan's face for
a bit longer. "Let's get you out of here and into a nice
cold cell."

Manuel and Susan followed Clint's lead, helping Rogan
to his feet and dragging him out through the front of the
bathhouse. Clint and Manuel each took one of Rogan's
arms and Susan held the gun on his back just in case he
got any wild hairs.

"You'd better pray we find Carmella real soon," Susan
told him. "Or I'll come back for you whether you're in a
cell or another state."

Rogan merely nodded. He didn't have anything left to
answer back to her threats, and it seemed as though it
took everything he had just to move his legs while being
dragged across the floor.

As they passed the front desk, Clint looked back to
Susan and quietly nodded toward the spot where Mario
was laying. She didn't have to be told to keep quiet as
she broke off from the others and went to tend to the old
man. That way, Rogan still thought he had someone following him with a gun on him even though it was just
him and the two men holding him up.

Clint and Manuel dragged Rogan to the jail, which was
a small building tucked away in a lot behind a guard station near the train depot. Since Los Rios Verdes was too
small to elect a sheriff, they relied on the railroad guards
to keep the peace and watch over the folks in the jailhouse.

At least, that was how Clint figured it worked. Like any
other small town, there was probably some system that
worked well enough for the amount of trouble Los Rios
Verdes saw. All that really mattered to Clint was that there

was someplace to dump Rogan once he was through carrying him.

The young man at the guard station took the gunman off of Clint's hands and told Clint something about the law coming through town every few days. Since he was probably paid through the railroad, the guard was much more concerned with the train and its station than he was with all the buildings behind it. Clint didn't worry too much about all of that, since Manuel jumped right in and explained his "business" to the guard.

"These are wanted men," Manuel said. "And they need to go to San Francisco in the morning to stand trial. My partner and I will take them ourselves, so just keep this one locked up for the night."

"Fine with me," the guard said. "Just so long as they don't cause any more trouble at this station."

"Don't worry about that. This is the liveliest of that bunch."

"Wait a minute," the guard said, suddenly perking up. "Did you say others? Where are they?"

"Dead," Clint said before Manuel could build up the story any more. "In the bathhouse. My friend here will clean them up for you, since he'll need to have them as proof to collect his reward. Isn't that right?"

"Sí, amigo. We'd better get started." Manuel made it perfectly clear that he was stressing the "We" part in that last sentence.

Clint wanted to argue, but decided Manuel had more than earned a helping hand from him. Besides, arguing with the Mexican would have taken more time than just doing the job and getting it over with. Clint went back to the bathhouse and Manuel ran to get his wagon.

It was a dirty job, but someone had to do it.

SIXTEEN

Clint was relieved to find Carmella sitting at her husband's side when he returned to the bathhouse. Susan was there, too, and was dabbing a wet cloth on the nasty looking bump that had already come up on the old man's head. The Italian couple seemed justifiably rattled, but otherwise in fairly good shape.

The moment she saw Clint walk in, Susan rushed over to him and spoke in a soft whisper directly into his ear. "I didn't let them go into the back room yet. Is someone going to get those bodies out of there soon?"

"Yeah," Clint said wearily. "Me and your boss."

"Isn't there an undertaker?"

"There isn't even a second street in this place, Susan. I was surprised there was a jail."

"Yeah, I guess you're right. One can always hope, though."

Looking over to Carmella, Clint asked, "Are you all right, ma'am?"

The old woman looked up at him, but didn't answer right away. She seemed too stunned to get her words together until she quickly nodded and put on a weak smile. "Yes, I am fine. Thank you for asking."

"Where were you when this happened?"

"I went to our home, which is just down the street behind the store. I heard someone say there was gunshots and prayed to God it was just someone having a fight in a saloon. But then I hear that the shots, they come from here. I wanted to run over here, but Alexander wouldn't let me."

Clint looked over to Susan with a questioning expression, but only got a confused shrug in response.

"Alexander?" Clint finally asked.

"He's the nice boy who brings us our food and helps around here sometimes. He told me to wait a little bit because the guards would probably come out to help soon. I tried to leave anyway, but he kept me there until the shooting was over."

Pushing down the impulse to go back to that guard station and give that kid a piece of his mind, Clint said, "That was the best thing you could have done. How are you doing?" he asked Mario.

"Eh, just a bump," the old man replied. "What about you?"

"I'm fine." Clint heard the wagon pull up outside and went to the window to take a look for himself. It was Manuel, and the Mexican seemed only too eager to come in and claim his bodies. "Why don't you two head back home and let us clean up a little," Clint said.

"I've seen blood before," Mario said. "I was in this country during the war, you know."

Clint listened to a few hazy stories as he and Susan helped the couple outside. Manuel stormed in and went straight to the back room, where he started in on his grisly chore.

When the couple was well on their way back to their home, Clint took Susan aside and asked her, "What about you? Are you all right?"

She took a deep breath, and when she exhaled, Susan

nodded. "Are you kidding me? Wrestling with you in that tub and then getting into a scrape like that right afterward has got my blood flowing. You'd better come find me when you're ready to turn in for the night."

Clint studied her when she spoke and was amazed to find that Susan seemed completely genuine in what she'd told him. In fact, she even let her hand slide between his legs for a moment before she turned and walked away.

If there was one thing that kept Clint in the life he'd chosen, it was the constant flow of surprises that kept coming his way. Just when he thought he'd figured the world out enough to get comfortable, something came along to shake things up. Sometimes, however, that something was a someone much like the shapely brown-haired lady who strutted away now, knowing full well that his eyes were glued to her swiveling backside.

Clint shook his head and laughed to himself. Manuel was already coming out of the bathhouse with Wade's body draped over his shoulders. He wore a greedy smirk as he stepped over to the wagon and unceremoniously dumped the corpse into the back.

Surely, Clint could have thought of a hundred better ways to spend an evening, but rather than choose any of those, he helped Manuel take the bodies from the bathhouse and drop them into the wagon. After that, he parted ways with the Mexican and headed back to the place where he'd rented a room for the night.

The moment Clint's head hit the pillow, it seemed as though the entire day caught up to him in a rush. His heart had been pounding so quickly with every kind of emotion that the inside of his body felt as though it had been put through a wringer. One by one, he let his muscles relax and a long breath slowly seep from his lungs. His eyes drooped shut through the entire process, and by the time they were closed, he let the last bit of the breath drift out of him.

The darkness inside his little room wrapped around him like a cool hand. Even the noises outside his window had died down a bit. Either that, or his ears were still ringing from all the gunshots that had been fired at and around him. Clint didn't really care which it was. All he did care about was that he could feel sleep creeping up on him, and he wasn't about to keep it back another moment longer.

At first, Clint didn't hear the knocking on his door.

When it came again, Clint heard it but decided to ignore it anyway.

The third time was a little louder and more insistent, so he grudgingly got to his feet and went to the door.

Susan was standing in the hall with an apologetic smile on her lips. "Mind if I come in?"

"Actually, I was just trying to get some sl—"

"That's fine," she interrupted, placing one hand flat on his chest so she could push him back inside as she stepped into the room. "You just lay right back down on that bed and we can sleep together."

"But I really need to sleep."

"Oh, you need me here, Clint. Look at yourself. You haven't even gotten out of your clothes yet. How are you supposed to sleep with all these clothes on?"

He'd barely even noticed, but Clint was still wearing everything except his boots when he'd dropped down onto the vaguely comfortable mattress. Even so, he struggled a bit at first when Susan began tugging at his shirt and pants. That was mainly because he could feel parts of him waking up again the moment her hands made contact with his skin.

"That's not so bad, now, is it?" she asked once she

pulled his clothes off and slid against his chest, arms, and back.

Clint watched her moving next to the bed, a ghostly, almost dreamlike figure shedding her clothes until her skin glistened in the pale light. "I guess it's not too bad," he said.

SEVENTEEN

The next morning came in little glimpses of light that invaded Clint's sleep beginning an hour or two before dawn. Most of the night sailed by in a deep, dreamless sleep, but once his body had rested up a bit, his senses regained their sharpness by the second.

And when his ears were able to pick up the sounds of the trains that rumbled through the nearby station, Clint's time for uninterrupted sleep was over. He'd been in towns that saw more trains than Los Rios Verdes, but he hadn't slept so close to a depot in a good, long while. That, added to the fact that there were hardly any other buildings to cushion the noise of the engines, made sleeping any longer a definite challenge.

Still, Clint did his best to squeeze in a few more hours of rest. The next time his eyes opened, it wasn't just because of the piercing shriek of a whistle and the roar of steam-powered wheels. There was something much closer to capture his attention. Namely, a warm, shapely body crawling on top of him like a stalking cat.

By the time Clint opened his eyes and was able to focus, most of the light was once again blocked from falling directly onto his face. Susan looked down at him with her hair spilling over her shoulders as her hands settled on either side of his head. Her legs closed in around his hips and slid luxuriously up against his skin.

"Good morning," she whispered.

"It feels like I just closed my eyes."

"Well, it's no use trying to get to sleep. The trains have been rolling in like clockwork and yours is due pretty soon, isn't it?"

Clint felt energy flowing through him as his blood pumped through his veins at a quickened pace. "Yes, it is, but we still have some time."

"Time? What for?"

"For this." With that, Clint reached up and wrapped both arms around her, pulling Susan down so that she was directly on top of him, with every inch of her body pressed against his.

She immediately kissed him passionately on the mouth. When she felt Clint's erection pushing against her, she shifted her weight and opened her legs just enough so that it fit nicely between her moist lips. Susan let out a contented sigh and closed her eyes as Clint pushed up inside of her. She lifted her upper body slightly using her arms, just enough to allow her to rock slowly back and forth.

With her naked body seeming to take up everything he could see or touch, Clint felt as though he was still dreaming, as he became enveloped by her warm body. She rode him until he took hold of her and rolled her onto her side. From there, he felt Susan's leg wrap around his hip, allowing him to enter her once again and continue the rhythm of their lovemaking.

Her hands slipped through his hair and over his face as she showered him with kisses. Her breath came in deepening gasps that began taking over her entire body as he thrust into her harder and harder.

Before long, Clint had both of his hands clenched in hers and had rolled beneath the covers until he was on top of her. The sheets twisted around them like a soft cocoon, stretching as he rose up over her pressing both of her hands firmly against the mattress.

Susan spread her legs open wide for him, locking her eyes onto his as he entered her with long, powerful thrusts. She opened her mouth as if she wanted to speak, but merely pushed her head back against the pillow and let out a moan that rumbled through the room just as the noise of a train whistle filled the air.

Acting as though they still had to keep quiet and hide what they were doing, Susan let her voice become louder only as the ruckus of an approaching train rumbled through the window. Her hips were pumping in time to Clint's, grinding against the slick surface of his cock until she felt it brush against just the right spot.

Clint pushed all the way inside of her and stayed put for a few moments, savoring the way she felt around him. Not only did he want to focus on how hot and warm it felt to be inside of her, but he also savored the feel of her naked skin against his stomach and arms. When she arched her back at the end of his thrusts, her erect nipples brushed against his chest, teasing him deliciously time and time again.

Opening his grasp, Clint slid his hands out of hers and moved his palms down the length of her arms and along the sides of her firm breasts. She breathed quickly and squirmed a little, but not enough to stop what he was doing.

As he moved his hands farther down her sides, Clint could feel the muscles between Susan's legs tightening around him, massaging his erection until it became even harder inside of her. Still moving his hands down over her, Clint got his legs beneath him and got up onto his knees. Both hands had slid around to cup her buttocks, lifting her up until her lower half was off the bed.

Holding her in his hands like that, Clint was able to

move her exactly the way he wanted when he once again began pumping in and out of her. Susan quickly learned to enjoy allowing him to have control of her, and reached both arms over her head to grab hold of the headboard.

She didn't wait for another train to come by before clenching her eyes tightly shut and letting out a moan that quickly became a lingering, passionate cry. Clint closed his eyes and listened to her, kneading her flesh through his fingers and allowing himself to be carried away by the pleasure that coursed through him.

His body began to come alive with the first hints of his climax, and Clint started pumping even harder between her legs to push himself over the edge. He didn't want to put it off any longer, and by the sound of Susan's cries, neither did she.

Suddenly, her eyes shot open and she propped herself up onto her elbows. She groaned every time he slammed against her now, and pushed her hips forward every time as well. Clint exploded inside of her with so much intensity that he grabbed her with all the strength in his body.

Susan responded by tossing her head back and stretching her entire body as her own orgasm made its way through every inch of her flesh.

Their climaxes seemed to make time stand still for a few moments, until the pleasure finally let go of them.

Finally, when Clint opened his eyes and took another breath, he saw Susan smiling back at him. Her hair was a tousled mess, and her face was glistening with a fine layer of perspiration.

"Well well," he said. "Good morning indeed."

EIGHTEEN

Clint had more than a few uncomfortable glances aimed in his direction as he stood on the train platform and said his good-byes to Manuel and Susan. Of course, that was probably due to the fact that Manuel didn't want to leave his wagon any longer than necessary and had pulled the load of corpses topped by his one live prisoner up to the wooden structure itself.

The bodies were covered by a tarp, but the smell was more than enough to announce what was under the cover. What little doubt there might have been was dispelled by the blood that had soaked through the material in some spots.

For his part, however, Manuel seemed to be in high spirits. He held the reins to his team in one hand and reached down with the other. "*Adios, amigo.* Time with you is never boring. Perhaps we'll meet up again soon, once both of us have some more money in our pockets."

Clint shook the hand Manuel offered and said, "I'd say you'll probably have more money than me. But since you're the one dragging those bodies all the way to San Francisco, I'd also say you earned every penny."

71

"You're damn right. And I'll buy a round of drinks to celebrate next time we meet. *Está bien?*"

"You bet, Manuel. That's fine with me."

Susan was standing next to the wagon, as though she wanted to be closer to Clint but didn't want to let Manuel get too far away either. "I'll be looking for you, Clint Adams. And when I find you, watch out."

Clint laughed and reached out to take her in his arms. "I'll try not to be too hard to find."

That was all they said to each other before pressing their lips together in a kiss that didn't end until the whistle of Clint's train blew for the third time. Reluctantly, they broke apart. Clint stepped back and enjoyed the view as Susan turned around and climbed onto the wagon. She and Manuel both raised their hands to wave before the Mexican snapped the reins and got the wagon moving away from the platform.

Clint walked over to where the livestock was being loaded onto the locomotive and patted Eclipse on the nose as the black Darley Arabian stallion was led onboard. It wasn't the first time the horse had been on a train, but it was plain to see that Eclipse would much rather run all the way to Sacramento.

At least, it was obvious to Clint.

"All aboard!" came the thundering voice of the conductor. "Final boarding call!"

Once he was sure that Eclipse was in good hands, Clint walked over to where the last couple of stragglers were stepping onto the passenger car and waited to get onboard. The train was fairly crowded, but Clint managed to find a seat on the right side of the car so he could watch Manuel drive away from town.

After one last blow of the whistle, the train huffed a couple of times and lurched into motion. From inside the passenger car, Los Rios Verdes looked even smaller than it did when he'd been walking through the middle of town. Even though he spotted a few more houses hidden behind the main row of businesses, it still looked like someone had sliced up a regular town like a pie and set down a single section next to the train tracks.

With the sun at just the right angle in the sky, Clint saw some of the light sparkling the winding rivers that must have been the namesake of the town. He was too far away to tell if the water looked green, but he didn't have any problem taking someone else's word for it.

The station was gone now and the train was still picking up speed as the other passengers were getting settled in their seats. Clint held his ticket in one hand when he saw the conductor walking down the aisle to collect them. While he waited, he looked out the window at the familiar wagon that Manuel was driving out of town.

At that moment, both the Mexican and Susan looked toward the train and started waving. Clint found himself returning the wave almost immediately. He knew the train was too far away for them to see him through the window, but that didn't really matter. It just seemed like the proper thing to do.

Manuel had never been the easiest guy to get along with, but he'd always proven to be an interesting fellow. If it wasn't one thing that was stirring up the Mexican's life, it was another, and he always had room for his friends when getting wrapped up in something new.

All in all, Clint was glad he'd met up with Manuel during his brief stay in Los Rios Verdes. Having Susan there as well had been an even more pleasant surprise, which made the short visit downright enjoyable. But as he always felt after meeting up with Manuel Ortiz, Clint was glad to be moving along.

Traveling in a wagon full of bodies might have been the Mexican's idea of an exciting time, but it sure as hell wasn't Clint's. Just thinking along those lines made the train's stiff-backed bench seem more and more comfortable.

"Tickets, please," the conductor said as he stepped up to Clint's row.

The portly man in the blue suit and round hat collected the tickets from the others nearby and turned to Clint with a well-worn smile.

Handing over his ticket, Clint asked, "How long before we get to Sacramento?"

"Should be there tomorrow afternoon."

"Great. Thanks."

Taking back his torn stub, Clint shifted down into his seat until his head could rest comfortably on the backrest. Of course, "comfort" was a relative term considering he was trying to relax on a bench made of wood, steel and the bare minimum of padding. But once he had something supporting his head, Clint pulled his hat down over his face, folded his hands over his stomach and closed his eyes.

As hard as the benches were, the motion of the train seemed to rock him back and forth until the uneven wooden slats became more than tolerable. On top of that, the rattle of wheels over the tracks, combined with the rush of cool air through the window, made it even easier for Clint to drift off into a light nap.

NINETEEN

Clint woke up to the sound of the train's whistle ripping through the air. The sounds made by the rumbling locomotive weren't anything new to him, but he'd been sleeping lightly enough for just about anything to jostle him out of his doze. Still a bit groggy, Clint tried to drift off again but was awakened again, this time by the sound of a baby who'd been startled by the whistle as well.

Knowing that the infant would probably be making a lot more noise than anything attached to the train, Clint abandoned the notion of getting any more sleep and sat up in his seat. After sliding his hat back onto his head and away from his face, he looked out the window while trying to work out some of the kinks from his neck and shoulders.

Spring would be coming soon, and he could see some hints of its arrival in the colors of the trees and landscape. No matter what season it was, the land outside the window at that particular moment would have been close to breathtaking. At that time, with traces of snow laced throughout some of the distant high country and the trees inching toward their greener buds, the view was closer to awe inspiring.

There wasn't anything as grand as a mountain range close enough to touch or a canyon that opened up like a gaping maw, but that didn't take anything away from what held Clint's eye. In fact, it was the simple beauty of the land that made him want to gaze out at it for hours on end. The only thing he could think of at that moment that would have been better was if he and Eclipse were riding out there on their own.

And just when he thought it couldn't get better, Clint pushed the window down some more and was treated to a gust of cool, rushing air. Despite the chill and occasional cinder that would be thrown off the wheels, the air rushing through the window pleased him, because it made almost enough noise to drown out the baby a couple rows over.

"Ahhh," came a voice from next to Clint. "That's better."

Clint turned around to see a man dressed in a dark blue suit, which even he could tell was expertly tailored. The man appeared to be in his late thirties or early forties, with a thin mustache and a pair of bushy sideburns to offset it.

The man pointed to the window and said, "I was going to ask you to do that earlier, but you were asleep. Too bad we can't get out there and walk around for a bit, eh?"

"I was just thinking that," Clint said. "It's some mighty nice country."

"Yes, it is, but I was referring to it more as an escape, if you know what I mean," the man added, nodding back toward the woman who was struggling to keep her child's growing tantrum under control.

Clint smiled and nodded. "You got a point there."

"I'm Marcus Kary," he said in a voice that sounded as though it couldn't be anything else but formal.

"Clint Adams."

Over the years, Clint had gotten very good at knowing whether or not someone recognized his name. Some would get a quick look of awe or fear. Others, like young gunfighters, would glare at him the way a hungry bear stares down its next meal. And then there were men like Marcus, who didn't have the faintest clue who Clint might be.

Many times, Clint wished there were more Marcus Karys in the world.

There wasn't much brute strength in Marcus's grip, but he shook Clint's hand with genuine gusto. "Pleased to meet you, Clint. Where you headed?"

"Sacramento."

"Really? Me, too. I'm going there on business."

Nodding, more out of politeness than anything else, Clint said, "Sounds interesting."

"It really is. I sell photography supplies and am meeting a man who's about to embark on an expedition to record the life of the Yokuts Indians. He'll be living among their tribe for six months, and that's not something that's normally allowed. Very fascinating indeed."

Hearing that, Clint couldn't help but smirk when he thought about how much the word "business" could entail. Just yesterday, Clint had been loading bodies onto a wagon for the sake of Manuel's business. He was delivering papers that had almost gotten him killed on account of his own business.

Judging by the excited gleam in Marcus's eyes, "fascinating" was another term that changed its definition depending on who was using it. Clint didn't want to be rude to the other man, though, and made sure his smile appeared to be more interested than amused.

"Have you ever been to Sacramento?" Marcus asked.

"Once or twice. It's been a while, though, so I'm sure a lot has changed."

"Maybe not as much as you'd think. I can tell you some points of interest if you'd like."

Clint winced when the screaming baby took a deep

breath and put every bit of energy its little body could muster into a scream that damn near rattled every window in the car. In fact, Clint swore he felt his eyeballs rattle inside their sockets before even half of the infant's breath had been expended.

"Does this train have a dining car?" Clint asked.

Marcus looked over his shoulder and pressed a finger against one of his ears. "I don't know, but I'd be willing to go up front and help shovel coal if it'll put some distance between me and that little . . ." Cutting himself off, Marcus shrugged and said, "Well the little guy's having a bad day. Let's give him some room."

"That's a very diplomatic way to put it," Clint replied.

"Diplomacy is a big part of any business. Well, the successful kind anyway. Wouldn't you agree?"

Clint nodded and followed Marcus to the narrow door at the front of the car. Perhaps all kinds of business did share things in common. The term "fascinating," on the other hand, was still debatable. Clint realized that as Marcus kept filling him in on every last "fascinating" detail regarding photography in daylight as opposed to artificial light.

Suddenly, the baby's screaming didn't seem so bad.

TWENTY

It didn't matter that Clint had taken much longer trips in his life. Whether it was by train or horseback, Clint had gone for weeks at a time in between stops, so he knew what it was like to travel over long distances. Compared to most of those longer trips, the train ride to Sacramento wasn't much more than a walk in a park.

But he'd never traveled with Marcus Kary on those other trips. If he had, Clint swore he would have either killed himself or the well-dressed businessman before they got halfway to their destination.

Marcus was a nice enough guy, but he simply never stopped talking, about every little thing that came to his mind. Even when Clint tried to get up and leave during one of the few times Marcus paused to take a breath, the other man simply agreed that stretching his legs was a wonderful idea and followed Clint wherever he went.

It had been entertaining when they ate their lunch in the dining car and also when they'd sat next to a pair of attractive sisters from New Orleans. But after several hours of nonstop chatter, ranging from such topics as Indian fishing customs to the migration habits of Alaskan crabs, Clint was fresh out of polite smiles and mindless nods.

The only break he got was when he found a space on a bench in another car and pretended to fall asleep. When the blessed silence settled over him and he opened his eyes, however, he found Marcus in the seat directly across the aisle from him, ready to pick up right where he'd left off.

Clint didn't like to keep close track of the time when he was on a train, simply because being able to see the time made its passage go by that much slower. Since he couldn't imagine how time could drag by any worse, Clint took the watch from his pocket and flicked it open to see how much longer he had to smile and nod.

"Aw Jesus," he said, even though he hadn't planned on saying it out loud.

Marcus seemed surprised by the sudden exclamation, but only pleasantly so. "What's the matter? Is your watch broken?"

"No," he said, shaking his head in disbelief that only three hours had gone by since he had first shaken Marcus's hand. "It's working just fine. I just can't believe what time it is, that's all."

"I know exactly how you feel. Time truly does fly when you're in such good company."

Clint knew he wanted to spare himself from another couple hours of listening to Marcus's chatter, but the other man had the look of a child waiting for his presents on Christmas morning. So rather than search for the peace and quiet that had to be somewhere on that train, Clint nodded and asked, "So what were you saying about over-exposure on indoor photography?"

"I'm so glad you asked!"

The rest after that was a barrage of facts and figures that were all backed by an impressive amount of evidence and proof. As Clint listened, he wandered around the train, moving from car to car, with Marcus following closely, as though he was attached by a leash. The train wasn't very big—just two passenger cars, the little dining car and the cramped balconies in between.

The infant had hit its stride in the first passenger car and was now screaming as though its life depended on it. The second car had been taken over by two families from Oregon who'd decided to strike up a feud to pass the time, and the dining car was a bustle of noisy activity from all the people who didn't want to be bothered by the first two groups.

In the end, Clint and Marcus wound up on the iron balcony in between the dining car and the car used for storage of supplies and coal. Clint smiled and watched the scenery flow by, listening to yet another of Marcus's long-winded explanations. After exploring the rest of the train, listening to technical photography jargon didn't seem too bad after all.

TWENTY-ONE

As the train pulled into Sacramento and came to a stop, Clint actually found himself waiting at the platform for Marcus to catch up to him. The well-dressed businessman hurried off the car with a bag tucked under each arm. He and Clint moved away from the train even farther once the feuding families began streaming off.

"It's been a pleasure, Mr. Adams," Marcus said, extending one hand as far as he could without dropping his bag. "Would you like me to write down some of those places I was telling you about?"

"Sure," Clint said, much to his own surprise. "That Chinese restaurant you mentioned sounds pretty good."

The directions were scribbled onto a notepad and then handed over to Clint. "Hope everything works out with your business here. Be careful around that Judge Warrick. He's a mean one sometimes."

Clint didn't remember mentioning the name of the judge that he was visiting, but Marcus hadn't just pulled it out of thin air. At least that showed Marcus really did listen on those few occasions he wasn't talking. "I will, Marcus. Take care."

Clint shook the other man's hand and collected his single bag from the pile that had been growing on the platform next to the storage car. From there, Clint walked to the rear of the train, where the livestock was kept. All he had to do was put his face near the open door and Eclipse almost thundered out to meet him.

"That one's mine," Clint told the animal handler, pointing to the Darley Arabian. "You know a place in town where I can put him up?"

"There's a stable not too far from the station here. That should do just fine."

"Much obliged." After a quick inspection, Clint could tell that the handler had taken decent care of Eclipse. For that, he tossed the worker a few extra coins and led the stallion in the direction the other man had pointed.

Clint hadn't even left the platform before he was taken aback by the difference he could feel in Sacramento as opposed to the feel of Los Rios Verdes. It was as though he could sense the buildings pressing in on him from all sides and could feel the population of the city surging around like he was standing in the middle of a rushing stream.

It exhilarated him on every level, sending a rush through his blood that could only come from being in a place so bustling with activity. As he walked down the street, Clint thought that he hadn't spent enough time in the bigger cities lately. There was a special kind of exhilaration that a man could only feel in the middle of a city. It had been a while, but Clint had felt it last in New York.

After finding the stable and putting up Eclipse for the night, Clint wandered the streets of Sacramento for a while to stretch his legs. It was late morning, and there were so many people out and about that Clint thought he might get swept away in all the commotion. Another big difference from the towns where he'd been staying lately was the appearance of the people around him.

Being not only in a large city, but also so close to the coast, the locals wore clothes that actually reflected recent trends in fashion. That was seen more so in the women, since men's fashion never strayed too far from the norm.

The women were dressed to impress and Clint was very impressed indeed. He tipped his hat to the ones who passed him by and got more than one encouraging glimpse for his trouble. It seemed that the local women were glad to see a man who didn't look like he spent his days behind a desk.

They looked at him with interested smiles, and the ones who traveled in small groups whispered among themselves as though Clint was some kind of wild animal who'd escaped from captivity. For his part, Clint didn't mind the glances one bit. In fact, he quickened his pace toward the courthouse so he could be done with his business and soak up some more of those glances.

Once he'd reminded himself of why he was in Sacramento to begin with, Clint's thoughts quickly turned back to business. The bundle of papers looked as though it had been run through a machine and trampled by a team of horses, but it was still in Clint's inner coat pocket. He patted his hand over the familiar bundle, just to make sure it was still there, as he arrived at the step leading up to the courthouse.

Clint made sure his hat was tilted at the proper angle and that every button was fastened so he looked his best before entering the stately building. Not that he was worried about impressing anyone, but Clint knew things tended to run much smoother with official types if a man looked the part.

With his shirt buttoned up to his neck and his coat hanging over the Colt, Clint looked about as official as he could manage without the help of a tailor. That was good enough for him, so he figured it would be good enough for anyone else as well. All that remained was for him to enter the courthouse, make his delivery, and be on his way.

Hopefully, things would go just that simply.

A pair of policemen stationed outside the front doors to the courthouse stopped Clint before he entered. The smaller of the two pointed toward his gun belt and said, "If you're armed, the weapon has to stay with us."

Clint held open his coat and let the lawman take his pistol. "I'm here to see Judge Warrick. Is he in?"

"Does he know you're coming?"

"He should be expecting me. My name's Clint Adams."

"He'll check with the secretary," the policeman said, without even looking toward the bigger lawman.

The other policeman was already moving, and he went over to where a clerk sat behind a neatly arranged desk. There were a few words, and then the secretary nodded.

"The judge is in session right now, Mr. Adams," the policeman said. "But you can wait in his chambers. Right this way."

Clint followed the other man into the courthouse. He truly did enjoy when things went smoothly for a change. He had to enjoy it, since it so rarely ever happened.

TWENTY-TWO

The judge's chambers were elegant and lavishly furnished. Clint wondered if Warrick was considered one of the best judges in the area or if all judges were treated so well. As he sat down in a plush chair cushioned in fine velvet, Clint thought about how judges sat up at the front of a courtroom like kings. With that frame of mind, the extravagant chambers didn't seem so out of place. He wondered if that was how the judges landed such pristine treatment.

If he was in the same situation, he guessed he wouldn't correct anyone who mistook him for a king, either.

"Judge Warrick will be with you as soon as possible," the policeman said. "It may be a while though."

"I don't mind waiting. As long as there's no screaming kids or photographers in here, I'll be fine."

The policeman nodded and left the room.

Clint found a comfortable spot next to a window and kicked back there, perfectly content to let time slip by waiting for the judge. The chambers were sealed tightly and gave him the most quiet he'd had in a real long time. In fact, he was almost disappointed when the door came open and a barrel-chested man with a full, well-groomed silvery beard stormed in.

"Clint Adams?" the big man said.

Reflexively, Clint got to his feet. "That's me."

Striding through the room as though he owned the entire building and pulling his arms out of a flowing black robe, he still thought it was necessary to announce, "I'm Judge Warrick." He shook Clint's hand with a solid grip and quickly reached for a box of cigars on his desk. "Care for one?"

"No thanks, Judge."

"Suit yourself." He wore a simple shirt and suit pants held up by suspenders beneath the robe and kicked his feet up onto his desk the moment his backside hit his chair.

Once the end of his cigar was lit, Judge Warrick lost his imperious manner and let out a long, smoky breath. "That's much better," he said.

Clint removed the bundle of papers he'd been carrying and set them onto the desk next to the judge's feet. "I believe these are for you."

"Ah yes. Let's have a look at those." The judge kept his cigar clenched between his teeth as he took the bundle and unfolded the papers so he could examine them one at a time. He grunted every so often as he checked them over. A smile crept onto his face right before he slapped them flat onto his desk.

"Remind me again why the sheriff didn't bring these to me? Or why he didn't have one of his deputies do it for him?"

"He was a little shorthanded, sir. I agreed to do the running for him to take some of the load off his back." Clint had had plenty of time to come up with several ways to answer that very question. It seemed that nothing else was necessary, however.

"You mean the sheriff was too damn lazy to come out

here? That's a first. I remember that he was particularly fond of his vacations paid for by the state."

Clint smirked and shrugged. "He's spending some time where he's needed at the moment. He said that this wouldn't be a problem."

"It's not a problem, Adams. I'm just glad I can get this paperwork pushed through at all. The men named in these warrants will become fugitives wanted by the federal marshals once I make them official. And believe me, Mr. Adams, these men could use a headache that size after the shit they've pulled."

"Actually, I wanted to talk to you about some of the men named there."

"Go ahead. I've got until the end of this cigar before I'm needed back at my bench. And don't worry," he added with a wink. "I'm an expert at making these things last."

"It's good news, really. You might not have to worry about some of those men." From there, Clint proceeded to fill the judge in on what had happened when Wade and his men had come to keep the paperwork from leaving Los Rios Verdes.

Judge Warrick listened to the story without interruption, savoring the cigar as it burned away between his teeth. When Clint was finished, Warrick swung his feet off his desk and stood up. "That's a hell of a story, Adams. Unfortunately, I can't look at it as more than that."

"I assure you, it's true, sir."

"And I'm not calling you a liar. I just need proof. I'm a judge, you know. We're sticklers for that sort of thing. I will tell you this, however. Your bounty hunter friend owes you one hell of a favor, since the rewards on these men might very well triple once the federals are after them.

"Also, the papers cover a dozen others that are just as bad as the four you mentioned. Some are worse, even.

But you did a good thing and just between you, me, and the fence post, I'd like to shake your hand." Judge Warrick did just that, clasping Clint's hand and shaking it with such vigor that he seemed to be trying to pull it off.

"You saved me the trouble of convicting those bastards, and you saved the state from paying for their trial. After serving so long where I see that kind of scum in my courtroom, I picked up a knack for spotting the blood on their hands. Killers have dead eyes, Adams. I'm sure you've seen eyes like that."

"I sure have."

Warrick leaned over the desk as though he was confiding in a drinking buddy and said, "Once I see those eyes, I hardly even bother listening to the damn lawyers. What's the use? I am glad that when the men in those warrants are caught, they'll be brought to me. I know how to deal with killers. They sure as hell lose their fucking smiles when they're standing at the gallows."

"It's a long way down," Clint said, more as a remembrance of the conversation Manuel had had with Rogan on the subject.

Judge Warrick was amused by that. "Yes it is, Mr. Adams. A long way down, indeed."

Clint surely did know what a killer's eyes looked like. The odd thing was that he felt like he was looking into a pair of them at that very moment.

TWENTY-THREE

When Clint walked out of the courthouse, he should have felt a weight lifted off his shoulders. After all, the job he'd promised to do had been done and the warrants were on their way to sealing the fate of several more outlaws who surely deserved whatever was coming to them. He'd even made a good impression on Judge Warrick, which was one of those things that was like money in the bank.

Clint wasn't the type of man to befriend people just to get them in his pocket, but knowing a judge like Warrick might come in handy some day. After all the things that had come to him over the years, Clint was more than aware of how every little conversation could tie into something else farther down the road.

That, however, was also a part of what was bothering him. As he'd sat in those chambers and talked to Judge Warrick, Clint got an uneasy feeling in his gut about the man. The term "hanging judge" was fairly common, and men like that had their place in a hard world. But they usually didn't work themselves up as high on the pecking order as someone in Warrick's position. But Warrick was most definitely a hanging judge. Clint hadn't met anyone else who fit the description quite so perfectly.

There was no doubt in his mind what would happen to those men once they were brought in front of the judge, either by Manuel or someone else tracking them down. For all Clint knew, every man whose name was on those warrants deserved to swing. He also knew that they deserved a fair trial, just like anyone else.

By the time that last thought crossed through his mind, Clint was across the street from the courthouse, looking around at the city, which stretched before him like an intricate puzzle. It was still fairly early in the day and there was plenty of Sacramento for him to explore.

The more he thought about what had happened over the last few days, the more Clint wanted to just put it all behind him. As always, he'd done the best he could with whatever the world had thrown at him. There wasn't much else that could be expected from any man, and considering what had been thrown his way, Clint thought he'd done pretty well.

Shaking his head as though he was clearing raindrops from his hat, Clint let out the breath he'd been holding, picked a direction and walked that way down the street. Warrick would do whatever he was going to do, Manuel would do whatever he wanted to do, and there wasn't much of anything Clint could do about either one.

That was the way things worked and that was the way they would stay. Trying to change too much around him was one of the things that got Clint into trouble. Perhaps it would be best for him to keep his nose out of trouble for once and just try to soak up some atmosphere in a city that had plenty to spare.

Clint spotted a street sign that was straight out of the directions Marcus had given him on the train. The restaurant the other man had gone on about should have been just a block or two away from where Clint was standing. To top it off, Clint's stomach was just starting to gurgle.

The moment he struck out toward the restaurant, Clint

felt that weight lift off of him. It was a great feeling and one that he didn't feel all too often. He found the restaurant with no trouble at all and ate a light meal at a table next to a window overlooking a pleasant piece of scenery.

Sitting by the window was another thing that he rarely did, since that would only make it easier for someone to take a shot at him before he could react. But he forced himself to sit there and look out at the world like a normal person living something close to a normal life. Once he got over the tension in his nerves and the instinct to put his back to a wall, he had to admit the view was very nice indeed.

For a moment, he felt like he was doing more than looking out at a city street. For a few minutes while he ate his food and drank his drink, he felt like he was looking in on a life that was so far behind him that he'd forgotten it was even there.

He wasn't Clint Adams.

He wasn't The Gunsmith.

He was just some man sitting at a table, eating a meal and watching the people walk by.

He knew he couldn't live like that forever, and doubted he would even if it was possible. But it was nice to pretend for a little while that his biggest problem was making ends meet rather than trying to dodge bullets. He even tried to think about what it would be like to walk around without the ever-present weight of the Colt hanging at his side.

Better not push it, Clint thought with a wary grin.

TWENTY-FOUR

The trail had been a long one, but it ended at a small house butting up against a large hill a half day's ride from any town. It wasn't a particularly impressive house and wasn't even big enough to hold more than one family. There was no barn or ranch nearby.

Just the house.

The house and possibly half a dozen armed, desperate men.

Manuel and Susan had followed every lead they'd collected and listened to every rumor concerning the whereabouts of the men who'd robbed that Wells Fargo money. They'd been hoping to catch sight of a familiar face in Los Rios Verdes, but nobody had shown up. And nobody was going to show up either, after Wade and his boys had been swept away like so much garbage.

The bodies still stank in the back of Manuel's wagon, but they weren't going anywhere. All that mattered was that there was enough of them left for someone to identify. The men in the nearby house, on the other hand, could pick up and leave at any moment.

Manuel crouched behind some shrubs with his gun drawn and his eyes glued to the lonely house. His ears were pricked up and waiting for any and every sound that could possibly be someone closing in on him. After the chase those robbers had given him so far, the Mexican had prepared himself for damn near anything.

There was a nearby snap as someone stepped on one of the twigs Manuel had scattered around his position. When he turned to get a look at who was coming, he immediately saw Susan approaching with her hands held in front of her.

"Don't shoot," she whispered. "It's me."

"How close did you get?" Manuel asked.

"Close enough to get a head count."

"And?"

Moving in next to Manuel, Susan drew her own gun and turned so she was facing the house as well. "And there's four of them inside."

"Only four?"

"That's all I could see. There could be some sleeping or hiding in dark rooms, but there's surely nobody outside I couldn't pick out. There's two men patrolling around the place."

"You're sure that's all?"

"Take a look for yourself," she shot back. "There's nowhere to hide out there unless they're willing to crawl on their bellies like snakes."

"You hid from them."

"And I crawled on my belly like a snake."

Both of them stopped talking at the same time and crouched down a little lower. They'd been on the trail for so long that their senses had become attuned to the same things. Every little noise that seemed out of place was noticed, and both of their hands tightened around their guns with the full expectation of using them.

After a few seconds had passed, they both relaxed a bit. But neither of them took their eyes away from that house or the shapes moving slowly around it.

"So there were four of them, huh?" Manuel asked.

"That's all I saw."

"All right, then. There's nowhere else for them to go without us seeing them."

"And they can't even start running without us being able to catch up to them and put them down."

Manuel turned to her and let a wide smile slide over his face. "I like the way you think, señorita. You ready to go in and clean that place out?"

"You bet. Those stinking bodies in the wagon aren't getting any fresher."

"I don't have to tell you about how dangerous these *pendejos* are. Watch your back and move slowly."

"We'll watch each other's backs, partner. Now let's go."

They gave each other one last look and then broke away from each other in a pattern that they'd gone over for the last day. From the moment they'd pulled out of Los Rios Verdes, they'd been preparing for this moment as best they could. Although their blood was pumping and their hearts were racing, they moved on toward the armed fugitives who they knew would kill to preserve their freedom.

Manuel had worked with Susan for long enough to take his eyes off of her and trust that she knew what to do when the moment of truth finally arrived. For her part, she had enough confidence in both of them that they could come through this alive.

After all, that gamble was at the heart of every bounty hunter's job. None of them had to be told that a fugitive would rather kill than be caught, because if a man had a price on his head, that meant he had nothing left to lose.

Both of the people creeping toward the house had plenty to lose. For the moment, however, they just had to put that out of their minds and concentrate only on what was directly in front of them. Susan kept herself so low that she almost disappeared within the high grass swaying around the house. Manuel cut to one side, which was thick with bushes and weeds. Most of the branches were still bare, but there were enough to provide some degree of cover.

Those bushes thinned out way before the house, but the Mexican would deal with that soon enough. For the moment, he found a good spot where he could stay out of sight, hunkered down and waiting.

From his position, he could see the house and could even catch the occasional glimpse of one of the two men circling it. He'd lost sight of Susan, but that was something he'd expected after he'd gotten his first look at the area.

Manuel was just starting to get anxious when he heard the rustle of movement and a muffled scream. That was followed by the thump of a body dropping to the ground and a whistle. Actually, it was two short whistles and one long.

Just as they'd agreed.

Responding to Susan's signal, Manuel moved forward and headed toward the other shape that was left near the house. The man had been walking around the building, but had stopped when he heard the last couple of sounds. For the moment, he was looking in the direction where he'd last seen his partner, holding his gun at the ready.

"Someone there?" the solitary man asked. "Did you find someone?"

Still moving forward in long, even steps, Manuel said, "*Sí*. He found someone."

The other man twisted around and fired off a shot from the rifle that was held at his hip level. As soon as the bullet left the barrel, he was levering in another round and bringing the rifle up to rest against his shoulder.

At that moment, there was the sound of a heavy footfall just behind the sentry. The man spun around again, this time making sure he was ready to put down whoever had been trying to sneak up on him. When he turned, he saw nothing behind him, even though the thump of something solid against the dirt still echoed in his ears.

He didn't see Susan pressing her stomach against the ground less than five yards away, and he didn't see the large rock she'd thrown to draw his attention. He heard another loud noise, however, which was the crack of Manuel's gun sending a bullet through his shoulder blade.

Another shot sounded; this one coming from Susan's pistol as she punched a hole through the man's gut.

That just left whoever was still inside the house as the only ones standing between the bounty hunters and their payday. So far, Manuel liked his odds.

TWENTY-FIVE

Sid Hogan wore his .38-caliber revolver strapped under his left arm in a holster that was tied tightly against his torso. His right hand hovered over the gun's handle as though he didn't know whether he should draw or run. His mind wavered back and forth as well, his decision becoming harder as more and more gunshots echoed from outside the house.

"What the hell's going on out there?" Sid asked.

Standing in the largest of the house's three rooms, Sid and his partner ducked a little lower every time they heard a shot outside. The other man was Pete Sanders, a man with a medium build and long arms, which tended to make him look a bit taller than his five feet ten inches. At the moment, however, he didn't look very tall at all kneeling against the wall next to a window.

"How the hell am I supposed to know what's going on out there?" Pete shouted. "Someone's shooting at us!"

As if responding to those words, the gunshots outside faded away, leaving only the faintest echoes to be heard rolling off into the distance. Pete looked over to Sid and then up at the window. Gathering up all his courage, Pete turned around to face the window and slowly lifted himself up so he could peek out through the glass.

"Do you see them?" Sid asked, referring to the two men who were supposed to be guarding the house.

Pete couldn't see every bit of land through the window, but he could see the body of one of the men who'd been patrolling the area only seconds ago. He dropped down into a low crouch so that his head was beneath the window once again. Raising his pistol and thumbing back the hammer, Pete began to rock back and forth on the balls of his feet.

"One of 'em's dead," Pete said. "I don't know which."

"Aw Jesus. Who's out there?"

"I don't know. Probably the same ones that were after us all through Oregon and Colorado."

Sid took a deep breath and waited for a few moments. It didn't take long before the silence outside became almost too much for him to bear. Although he didn't fancy the idea of getting shot, he was starting to dread every moment of uncertain quiet that passed. He felt something bump against his back, but quickly realized that it was the wall and that he'd been shuffling in that direction without even knowing it.

"Then I say we end it," Sid announced in a cold, yet determined voice. "Right here. Right now."

Pete nodded once, as though he'd just had his fate decided in that one sentence. Although there still were no more shots coming from outside, he felt as though a war was raging around him. Without making another sound, he pointed first to Sid and then to the front. He then signaled that he was going to head toward the back of the house.

Acknowledging the simple instructions, Sid kept his head down and made his way slowly toward the front door. Just as he was reaching out toward the handle, he heard something move outside. He turned to look back into the room, but Pete had already gone. That just left him to deal with whatever was on the other side of that door. Based on what he'd seen and heard, he doubted he would like what he found.

Manuel kept his eyes focused on the house, but made sure Susan was visible in the edge of his field of vision. It seemed that she was right in saying that there were only the two outside guards, because the only movement once those two had been shot was the weeds bending in the wind.

Crouching down over the closest body, Manuel took a look for himself at the dead man's face. His heart beat a little faster, just as it always did when he took down a valuable target, but immediately sank when he took in the other man's features.

He didn't recognize him.

Every face looked different when compared to the drawings on wanted posters, and even more different when twisted in death. But the man laying on the ground at his feet didn't strike a chord in Manuel's mind. Not even in the least.

Since Susan was working her way around the house, Manuel kept moving as well. He headed over to the second guard, who was the one who'd actually gotten off a couple shots at the two bounty hunters. Trying to ignore the sick feeling in his gut, Manuel waited until he was right next to the body before he took a look.

Manuel let out the breath he'd been holding in a quick, relieved exhale. All he needed was a glance to recognize the face on that dead man. It was one of the robbers they were after. No question about it. Perhaps they'd taken on more hands, or perhaps the first man simply had been mistaken for someone else when the poster was made. Whatever the explanation, Manuel didn't concern himself with it anymore.

These were the men they were after.

That certainty allowed him to breathe a hell of a lot easier. After all, a case of mistaken identity for a bounty hunter could mean the difference between his next payday and being tried for murder himself.

Manuel wasn't sure how long he'd been examining those dead faces, but it felt like a whole new day when he looked up at that house again. He was just in time to see Susan sneaking around the back. She'd waited until he looked up at her before moving around to get into position.

Just like they'd planned.

Feeling the confidence pumping through him like liquid fire, Manuel quickened his pace toward the front of the house. He stopped short of walking straight up to the front door and cut sharply to one side to avoid putting himself directly in front of a window.

With his senses at their peak performance and searching for any little thing that might be out of place, he actually felt the twig beneath his boot as his foot lowered down onto it.

TWENTY-SIX

He knew firsthand that a man could hear and see an awful lot when his life was at stake, and when he stepped on that dry twig, he thought his life might very well be over. Manuel even felt a rush of thoughts flow through his head in the split second before the twig broke and made the sound that he'd been trying so hard to avoid.

As much as he wanted to think that he had things under control and that he could handle whatever came his way, the Mexican simply knew that taking the wrong step at that moment could be the last thing he did. That suspicion was confirmed as a gunshot exploded from inside the house and punched a hole through the front door.

The world tilted crazily around Manuel's eyes and ears, as though he'd lost his balance when trying to stand in the back of a speeding wagon. He felt as though he was falling, and wondered if he might be dead by the time he finally came down.

All of that happened in the blink of an eye, and by the time his eyes opened again, Manuel was on the ground and the world was moving at its normal pace again. Another shot had blasted through the door, but missed him by several feet as it hissed through the air above him.

Manuel took a moment to look around, which was when he felt the hard earth against his shoulder blades and the dull pain pounding through his back and ribs. He'd dropped down to the ground when he'd heard the first shot. That was all. He'd let his instincts take over and dropped.

A quick check was all he needed to confirm that he hadn't been hit, although he was still aching from his rough landing. Still moving on instinct, Manuel rolled toward the house as a third shot punched through the door in front of him.

He waited until there was a break in the gunshots before pulling his legs up underneath him and preparing himself to make a move. Knowing better than to make the same mistake twice, he looked quickly on the ground in his path and picked out the spots to avoid if he wanted to keep from announcing his position again.

The echo of gunfire was still rolling in the distance, but it seemed as though the person who'd been firing was taking a short breather. That was all Manuel needed to get him up and moving. He kept himself hunched over and pushed off with his legs, practically dancing between a small pile of dead leaves. Jumping over the small step leading up to the front door, he landed between the entrance and the closest window.

Manuel fought back the impulse to press his back against the wall, and instead placed the fingertips of his left hand against the house to steady himself as he settled beneath the sill. Now that he'd stopped moving, he could hear the person moving inside the house. A satisfied grin slipped across his face and he gripped his gun a little tighter.

That was much better.

Now that he was the one who could remain quiet while listening to what was going on, Manuel felt like he'd wrestled back some of the control. He wasn't stupid enough to let himself get too confident, however. That was a good way to get himself killed.

The only thing that kept him from charging into the house was the lack of sound coming from the back. He knew Susan was getting herself into position as well, and he wasn't about to spoil a perfectly good plan by jumping the gun just yet.

It pained him to keep himself in check, but Manuel did just that, and gave his partner another couple seconds to make her move.

Susan heard the shots coming from the front of the house and reflexively ducked low just in case one of those bullets was headed in her direction. It didn't take long for her to realize that she wasn't the target of that particular barrage, although her instincts remained to keep still and wait for the noise to pass.

But someone in her line of work couldn't afford to listen to every instinct. After all, the rational thing to do in that very situation was to point herself in the opposite direction and start running. It might not have been the most courageous or exciting thing to do, but it was rational as all hell. She swallowed her more rational instincts and kept moving, hoping that Manuel could handle whatever trouble came his way.

She was working her way around the house, looking for a rear entrance into the place. If she couldn't find a back door, she would have to make do with a window. Before she thought for too long about climbing through a frame of broken glass, she rounded the corner and spotted the narrow door at the back corner of the little building.

It barely looked like a regular sized door and had probably been built as more of an afterthought. She made her way to the door with her gun in one hand and her other stretching out toward the handle. Hoping to take advantage of the ruckus stirred up by that last round of shots,

Susan quickened her steps over the packed dirt.

Since the house was the only man-made object for miles, the sound of boots on floorboards was unmistakable. It rang through her ears like the sound of water dripping in an otherwise lifeless cave. There were a few people moving about inside the house and at least one that had to be close to the back door. She kept on moving anyway, letting her hand turn the pistol until it was pointed at the door.

She stood with her feet rooted to the ground, her finger curling around the trigger and her free hand resting on the door handle. The shots up front had stopped, leaving the footsteps as the only sound Susan could hear. Since she was paying such close attention, those steps seemed like the only sounds in Susan's entire world.

Knowing that Manuel was ticking off the seconds in his mind just as she was doing in hers, Susan waited until the proper time before making her play. Unfortunately, things didn't always go according to plan, and moments before she made her move, Susan was nearly knocked off her feet when the door flew open and chaos exploded in every direction.

TWENTY-SEVEN

The only thing Manuel had to do to unleash the hellfire was peek his head up to take a look through the window. He knew it was going to be risky, but he simply couldn't afford to go into that house completely blind. He did manage to catch a glimpse of someone standing no more than a foot from the glass, aiming as though he knew what was coming.

Manuel's reflexes kicked in and tensed every muscle in his body to try and clear away from the window before it was too late, and he managed to do just that with half a second to spare. Explosions thundered through the air and bullets shattered the window, showering glass down on the top of his hat.

It was too late to go back now, so Manuel did the only thing he could and charged forward. It no longer mattered if that was the smartest or even the best thing to do. That was simply the only option left open to him, because nobody was going to walk away from this unscathed.

It was too late for that.

Not knowing exactly what was waiting for him on the other side of that door, Manuel smashed his shoulder against it with every bit of his weight behind it. His feet pushed him onward as if there was nothing in his way and his momentum picked up where his own strength left off.

In a matter of seconds, he was inside the house and ready to face whatever was there. Deep down inside, Manuel had to admit one thing. This was his favorite part of the business.

The back door flew open as though a raging gust of wind had blown up from within the house. It swung out with such force that Susan wondered if her hand would still be attached to her arm as she pulled it away. Every part of her was intact, however, but she knew better than to assume that would last for very long.

Susan stumbled backward and might have fallen on her backside if she hadn't twisted her body at the last moment so that she bumped against the house instead. All the while, her gun remained pointed at the door, not moving until the figure who'd opened it flew outside in a blur of motion.

The only thing she saw was a human shape covered in dark clothes. An overcoat flowed out behind the figure like folded wings or a smoke trail as the person turned in mid-step to face her. Susan squeezed her trigger without even having to think about it. Although the action was as much a reflex as her breathing, she had enough control of herself to keep from emptying her pistol. Once the gun bucked in her hand, she fought to get a better look at the figure dressed in the dark clothes.

She knew she'd missed the man. In fact, she expected to miss, since she'd only fired to make sure that she wasn't an easy target. But the man didn't seem at all interested in returning fire. On the contrary, he turned sharply toward the surrounding bushes and headed for the trees just beyond them.

Susan had to admit that the man running from her without so much as a fight was the one thing she had least expected. Using her free hand and backside to push off the building, she launched herself after the man, knowing full well that she could outrun him. Just as she picked up steam, she felt her guts twist and her heart stop when the man stopped and twisted around on the balls of his feet.

"Goddammit," she snarled to herself when she saw the gun in the man's hand. Susan was more angry at herself, since she had known he was going to take a shot at her, but still let herself get caught flatfooted anyway.

But the time for regrets was later. The time for action was now. Still barreling forward, she dropped herself toward the ground with both hands outstretched. Her palms slammed against the dirt just as the man in front of her pulled his trigger.

He was a hell of a shot, because he almost hit her, even after Susan had dropped and started rolling to one side. That impressed the hell out of her since he was still twisting and skidding with his own momentum. Lead whipped past her head with inches to spare, quickly followed by another shot.

Susan was already rolling on the ground, pushing off with her arms and legs in a desperate attempt to steer herself away from the man shooting at her. The second bullet gave a high-pitched whining sound as it came at her, announcing its presence just before she felt the hot sting of skin and muscle being ripped from her left shoulder.

She came to a stop on her side, but was still able to pick out the silhouette of the man several yards away. Pointing her gun and pulling her trigger, Susan aimed more with her eyes on her target than by sighting down the barrel. Although she had no way of telling if she hit her target or even got close, her shot was enough to get the man moving again, and he took off for the distant trees.

Susan could feel the blood soaking into her collar in a warm flow. Her hand began to tremble slightly as she held the gun and aimed properly before taking one last shot at the fleeing man. Even though she knew the man was probably out of range, she fired anyway, just to make herself feel as though she'd done all she could.

From there, she got back up onto her feet and touched her fingers to the wound she'd just received. The rip in her flesh was more in her neck than her shoulder, but she could tell that the bullet hadn't hit anything vital, since she could still walk, see and move fairly well. Deciding to count her blessings later, she turned toward the house and started running back to see if Manuel needed any help.

Before she'd gone more than four steps in that direction, she spotted something on the ground that caught her eye simply because the dirt was all but barren except for a few scraggly weeds and pebbles. It was a bundle wrapped in burlap and tied together with twine. Because the bundle was laying on top of one of the footprints left by the man in the dark coat, her tracking instincts told her that the bundle hadn't been there before the man ran by.

Susan knelt down to examine the ground a bit further, just to make sure that her assumption was correct. After all, it didn't take long for tracks to get altered just enough to mar their true meaning. It didn't take much to see that she'd been right. The tracks did belong to that man, and the bundle had been dropped on top of them. Since the bundle wasn't hers, Susan knew it had belonged to the man in the coat.

As much as she wanted to open that bundle right there, she stuffed it into her pocket and rushed toward the house.

As Manuel charged into the house, he fired his gun to clear the way, entering the doorway through a cloud of gritty smoke. His face was twisted into a smile, as though he'd already bagged the man he was after, but that smile quickly faded once he saw what was waiting for him inside.

His shot hadn't hit a damn thing, since there wasn't anything in front of him apart from the opposite wall. The only other person inside the front room was huddled against the wall close to the window. His gun was in his hand and pointed toward the door, just waiting for a clear shot.

By stepping through the doorway and running inside with gun blazing, Manuel had given him the clearest shot any man could ask for. He realized his mistake the moment he spotted where the man was waiting. The fact that he was already staring down the barrel of the man's gun didn't help matters either.

Manuel braced himself for that other gun to go off in his face, even as he snapped his own pistol around and shouted, "Drop it or you're dead!"

TWENTY-EIGHT

Clint had been in Sacramento for close to five days before he saw a familiar face. Well, perhaps that wasn't completely true, since he did see Judge Warrick and one of the policemen every now and then, whenever he walked near the courthouse. It had been going on five days before Clint saw a friendly familiar face, and that face belonged to Susan Connover.

At first, Clint thought his eyes were playing tricks on him, but another glance or two thrown in the brown-haired woman's direction confirmed that it was indeed Susan. He'd been about to cross the street to a particularly good restaurant when he spotted Susan at the corner. Her long brown hair was tied back behind her head and her pretty face looked a bit worried, but it was her, all right. The shapely figure beneath the man's shirt gave her away.

Deciding to have a little fun, Clint fell in step with the flow of foot traffic on the side of the street and hid among those people until he got up close and behind her. Since Susan was staring intently down the street toward the courthouse, Clint had no trouble at all closing the distance between them until he could walk right up behind her.

He kept his steps light upon the boardwalk until he was

close enough to reach out and touch the back of her head. Instead of doing that, however, he stretched out both arms with his hands open, until finally sliding his fingers over her sides to tickle her ribs.

Although he'd been expecting her to jump or even let out a little surprised scream, Clint hadn't been expecting her to go for her gun. Her hand dropped down to the holster on her hip and drew her pistol before she even got a look at Clint's face. In one quick motion, she spun around, knocked Clint's hands away and jabbed the pistol's barrel into his gut.

Clint might have been taken by surprise, but his reflexes weren't exactly dead, either. The instant he felt the steel press against his belly, he dropped his hand down to take hold of the gun and twist it sharply in her grasp. Susan's fingers got pinched within the trigger guard once the barrel was pointing safely to the sky and soon the gun was out of her grasp completely.

"I know you're not exactly the dainty type," Clint said with a wary smile. "But aren't you a bit jumpy?"

It took a moment for the anger to drain out of her face, but Susan began to calm down the moment she got a look at who'd snuck up behind her. "Jesus Christ, Clint, you nearly scared me half to death."

Holding the gun between them, Clint answered, "Looks to me like I was closer to death than you."

"The gun has to be in my hand for you to be in any trouble. Speaking of that . . ." Susan snapped her hand out and reclaimed her weapon. As soon as the pistol was in her grasp, she dropped it back into her holster and secured it in place.

"I thought you and Manuel were headed to San Francisco."

"Not anymore," Susan said. "The warrants for our train robbers were handed over to the U.S. Marshals, and Sacramento is the closest federal courthouse from where we were."

"I'm surprised you had enough time to hear about the warrant changing."

"Manuel keeps up on those things. It's his business." When she said that last part, Susan changed the tone in her voice to mimic the Mexican just enough for Clint to know what she was doing. "I sure don't mind. It's a shorter ride and more money for both of us."

"Well, if you see Judge Warrick, send him my best."

"Do you know someone every place you go? Or are you just trying to impress me?"

Clint brushed the side of his hand along Susan's chin and said, "Maybe a little of both."

"I'm not exactly the type to blush, but you just got a lot closer than most men who try that sort of thing."

"I'll take that as a compliment."

"You better."

Now that he could feel that most of the tension was gone from her manner, Clint steered the conversation back onto the track he wanted it on.

"It sounds like everything is going well for the both of you. Why so jumpy, then?"

It was plain to see that Susan wanted to answer that question, but she stopped and glanced around nervously. Clint recognized the uneasiness in those eyes and didn't like it one bit. In fact, he even caught himself glancing around in the same direction that she had, as if he was looking for someone stalking him as well.

"Who's after you?" he asked.

"Maybe nobody."

"Or maybe somebody. Tell me who it is."

She took hold of his wrist and pulled him toward a small storefront. "Let's get somewhere off the street. I'd feel a whole lot more comfortable."

"That's strange, because I just got a feeling that was

anything but comfortable when I heard you say that."

She laughed at the comment, but it was still more of a nervous laugh than anything close to humorous. The place she led him served hot drinks at little round tables and had wide open windows that looked out onto the street.

A tea room.

That's what the place was called.

It had been so long since Clint had been into a place that didn't serve beer or steak that he'd almost forgotten the name for it.

Susan took a seat at a table in the window and moved her chair so that she could keep her eyes on the section of the street she'd been watching while she was outside. Clint got himself situated next to her. Although he felt like he was on display behind all that glass, it helped a bit that he could see everyone walking by.

"All right," he said. "We've got our seats and you can watch the street. How about you tell me what's gotten you so worked up."

Reaching into her jacket pocket, Susan fished out a small bundle of burlap wrapped up with twine. "It's this," she said, placing the bundle in the middle of the table.

TWENTY-NINE

Clint took the bundle in both hands and held onto it for a few moments, as though he didn't know quite what to do with it. After seeing the reaction the thing had gotten from someone like Susan Connover, he almost expected there to be something terrible inside that burlap. At the very least, he figured it had to be something worth the buildup she'd given it.

"Open it," she prodded. The expression on her face was full of anticipation, and she was literally on the edge of her seat as he pulled apart the twine.

Stopping before peeling back the flap of burlap, Clint asked, "Haven't you looked in here yet?"

"Of course I have."

"All right. Just checking." He continued to remove all of the twine, until the burlap was loose and practically falling apart. Feeling as though not only Susan but the entire room was looking intently at the bundle, Clint finally pulled it open to reveal what was inside. He was almost disappointed to find a collection of trinkets ranging from jewelry to personal items like money clips and a small match safe.

"Is this a joke?" Clint asked.

"Do you know anything about that train robbery that Manuel was telling you about before?"

"I heard about it, but not much really. Just that it happened and that it was pretty bloody."

"Well, nobody knew who'd done it at first, but the robbers were tracked down because of some things they took from the people they killed."

"This stuff?" Clint said, holding the bundle slightly off the table.

She nodded gravely. "See that money clip? The initials on there are the same as a banker's who was riding on the train. Also, two of those rings are part of a set taken from a woman visiting from England. The papers wrote about that, too, and Manuel told me about it since that jewelry was worth so damn much.

"The third ring in the set was found in a hotel in Utah, which is where the whole hunt for those men started. Until then, the law didn't rightly know who'd pulled that robbery. But once they found something linking the man who'd stayed in that room directly to that train, all they had to do was question the hotel clerk."

Clint laughed and shook his head. "Finding these assholes is never as hard as some people make it out to be. Half the time, they mess up so much you'd swear they wanted to be caught. The real trick comes in outfighting them once they've got their backs to the wall."

Setting down the bundle, Clint took a close look at Susan's face. That's when he noticed the bandage wrapped around her neck and poking out from beneath the open collar of her shirt. "Speaking of which, it looks like you managed to catch someone in a place they didn't like too much."

Susan looked back at him and then saw him pointing toward her neck. She touched the bandages herself and shrugged. "It's not that bad, but you're right." From there, she went on to tell him about her and Manuel's confrontation at the secluded house where they'd found Sid Hogan.

"Sid Hogan," Clint repeated. "That name sounds familiar. That's the one that robbed that train, right? Or at least one of them, anyway."

"Yeah. That's him all right."

"And he's the same one you brought in with Manuel?"

"Yep."

After a few silent moments had passed by, Clint looked around and even glanced out at the street where he'd found Susan. "So why aren't you in a better mood? Shouldn't you and Manuel be celebrating?"

"I didn't find this bundle on Sid Hogan."

"That's right. You said it was dropped by that guy that managed to give you the slip. Don't feel too bad about that. It happens to the best of us."

"That's what Manuel said. Hell, that's even what I thought until the ride here where me and Manuel got a chance to go over everything more carefully." She looked into his eyes and leaned forward so she could lower her voice and still be heard. "There's a lot that doesn't match up, Clint. So much that I start to get sick when I think about it."

"What doesn't match up?"

"First of all," she said, holding her hand out so she could tick off her points on her fingers. "That man that I chased down. He could have killed me. I know it. I feel it in my bones."

"And you may be right," Clint replied. "Funny things happen when the lead starts to fly. Sometimes it feels more like luck that keeps you alive than anything else."

"It's not that, Clint. He could have shot me down, but just . . . didn't. I know he could have killed me, but he didn't. It's almost as though he wanted to keep me alive."

Clint could have showered Susan with plenty of strange stories about odd things that had happened to him under fire. But since he could tell that none of them would have done anything but waste time, he kept them to himself and let her continue uninterrupted.

"Second, there's this bundle. If someone would go through all the trouble of robbing a train and everyone on it, why be so careless that you drop valuable things like these?"

"I'm telling you, Susan. Just because a man is mean doesn't make him smart as well."

"It's like a trail of bread crumbs, and without it, nobody would really know where to start in finding these men. It's too perfect and too fortunate of a thing to happen just on its own. I'm a God-fearing woman, but not even the Lord hands over people like this."

Clint could start to see where she was headed, but wasn't completely convinced. Not yet, anyway. "Go on," he told her.

Ticking off her third finger, she said, "When I got back into the house and found Manuel, Sid said we had to have gotten through nine men to get to him. I don't remember exactly when he said it, but that number nine sticks in my head."

"You and Manuel only found two men guarding the house, right?"

She nodded.

"And how many were inside?"

"Just Sid and the one that got away."

"You two checked that place once the smoke had cleared?" he asked.

"Even before the smoke cleared, and not only was there nobody else in there, but there wasn't even any place for someone to hide. The house was abandoned and built on solid ground. No cellar. No attic. Nobody else except for those two."

"That is strange, but I still don't see why you're so jumpy."

"I was waiting for Manuel," she told him. "And the more I was thinking about everything, the more I thought that there's still a big danger for both of us out there."

"You're talking about that fellow that got away from you." Susan nodded. "I didn't recognize his face from any bounty notice, but Sid's face and some of his men were plastered all over the place. There's something that just gives me a bad feeling. It's like the wrong man got away."

THIRTY

"Where are these men you captured now?"

"Manuel took them in to the law to claim our reward."

"Then that should wrap up the last of your questions."

"Yeah," she said rather unconvincingly. "I guess." Suddenly, her face brightened up a bit and her eyes focused on something outside on the street.

Clint followed her line of sight until it brought him to a familiar face making its way through the milling crowd. For a man who'd just gotten back from cashing in on a major payday, Manuel didn't look all that happy. In fact, he looked downright miserable, which tied a knot in the middle of Clint's stomach.

Neither of them said a word to each other until Manuel spotted Susan in the window of the restaurant. Once the Mexican joined them at their table, quick greetings were exchanged and all three of them got right back to business.

"So tell me what you think about all of this," Clint said to Manuel. "I heard about what happened from Susan and it does seem a little peculiar, but not so much that I'd lose much sleep over it."

Manuel shook his head and let out a troubled sigh. "It

is strange, amigo. But I would have been happy to just take the money and run if Connover here didn't keep making me think about everything. There was one thing in particular that makes me wonder.

"When I was in that house, Sid had the drop on me. There's no question about that. He didn't fire, though. I could see it in his eyes that he just didn't have it in him. Those weren't the eyes of a killer, amigo. Especially not the killer of innocent men and women like the man that robbed that train."

Clint nodded, taking in the story without interrupting. So far, the main thing that worried him was the way Manuel and Susan were acting. He'd only known Susan for a little while, but this was all way out of Manuel's character.

"On the way here, I talked with Sid Hogan and asked about the things he'd done." Leaning in, Manuel looked Clint straight in the eyes and said, "He didn't know a damn thing about that train robbery."

"What?"

"He and some of his men had robbed a few general stores, but nothing too serious. He'd even killed a man, but nothing like the blood that was spilled on that train."

"And how do you know all this?" Clint asked. "Because he told you so? Pardon me if I don't take those words as gospel."

"Connover and I have been on this trail for some time now. Looking back on it, it's easy to see how it was a little easier than it should have been." He looked a little embarrassed when he added, "We barely had to do much more than follow the hints that were left for us. The hardest part was trying to keep ahead of the other bounty hunters who nearly got there before we did."

"Those men guarding the house were nothing," Susan said. "They were hired guns, but not the kind that could have pulled off that train robbery."

"So what does all of this lead to?" Clint asked, even though he had a good idea of what the answer would be.

Manuel reached into the inner pocket of his jacket and pulled out a piece of thick paper that was frayed at the edges and folded into quarters. "It leads right here, amigo," he said, unfolding the paper and placing it flat onto the table.

Clint looked down at the paper and saw a wanted poster offering the reward of $5,000 for the capture of "the men responsible" for the train robbery in question. Even without any names mentioned, there was a rough drawing of a few of the men with one singled out as "possible leader." It was more than three months old.

"This is the first reward offered for those killers," Manuel explained. "I found this a week before I met up with Connover and kept it. I think this is one of the first notices put up about this reward. Here's a newer one." With that, Manuel peeled back the poster to reveal that it had actually been two pieces of paper folded together.

The second notice wasn't as frayed and still had the color of newer paper. The sum had increased by $3,000 and now also mentioned that there was a gang of "up to ten armed men" along with the leader, who was now named as Sid Hogan. The picture of Sid was clearer, yet still bore a resemblance to the picture on the first poster.

"All right," Clint said. "What am I supposed to be seeing?"

"This here," Susan said, tapping the picture on the newer poster, "is Sid Hogan. This one," she said, tapping the picture on the older notice, "isn't."

Clint looked back and forth between the two pictures and then shrugged. "It could be."

"Sure, it could be," Susan replied. "But this first picture is the man who got away from me outside that house. He looked similar to Sid Hogan, but only at a quick glance. Having seen both of them up close, I know these drawings are of two different men. This is what gives them away."

Looking down at where Susan was pointing, Clint could see she was showing him a scar on the chin of the subject of the first picture. Sure enough, that scar wasn't there on the second picture.

"I take it the man that got away had that scar?" Clint asked.

Susan nodded without hesitation.

"And Sid doesn't?"

Both of the bounty hunters shook their heads at that one.

"Did you mention any of this to the law, Manuel?"

"*Sí, amigo.* But they just handed out the money and sent a wire off to Wells Fargo. The U.S. Marshal here seemed more anxious to please them than listen to me."

"Is there at least going to be a trial?" Clint asked.

Manuel nodded. "Four days from now. Sid will be brought up in front of Judge Warrick."

"Judge Warrick? Maybe I ought to have a talk with this Sid Hogan myself. Something tells me your prisoner, innocent or not, is being fitted for a noose already."

THIRTY-ONE

Even with the weight that was resting heavily on his shoulders, Manuel seemed to get a genuine thrill out of being the one to escort Clint in to see Sid Hogan in his cell. Since he'd been the one to speak with the marshals and hand over the prisoner, Manuel didn't have too hard of a time getting Clint in to have a talk with Sid.

"Be quick about it," the marshal had told them.

The talk was quick indeed, simply because Clint didn't need much time to size up Sid Hogan. The man he saw in the cell was not only scared, but utterly petrified. When asked about specific details regarding the train robbery, Hogan truly didn't know the answers.

More than once, the prisoner tried to lie just to end the questioning, but Clint picked up on that right away. Clint had sat in on too many poker games to be fooled so easily, and Sid was too scared to do a very good job of lying. Those elements combined to give Clint what he was after without very much fuss at all.

It was over in a matter of minutes, and when Clint turned around to leave, he could feel the relief coming from the man in the cell. He didn't say a word to Manuel as he and the Mexican were shown out. Clint even let

Manuel handle the marshal as more details about the trial were discussed and good-byes were said.

Once they were back on the street, Manuel looked at Clint and asked, "What do you think?"

"If I had to wager on it, I'd say you've got a good knack for reading people. There might be a problem after all."

"You think he's innocent?"

"That's a bit much for me to decide. He's guilty of some things, even he's admitted that. But this train robbery and all those murders? I'm having a hard time swallowing that."

For a moment, Manuel looked proud of himself that his conclusions had been given a bit of merit. But the satisfied grin quickly faded and he asked, "So what now? Try to get those marshals to let him go?"

Clint couldn't help but give a laugh at that. "You think you're the only one getting a reward from this? The marshal in there is the one who gets to hand Wells Fargo their killer, and there's a lot that comes along with that. But there's one thing in particular that gets under my skin about all of this. The money. Where's all that money that was stolen?"

"We searched every man and every inch of that house," Manuel said. "There was no money."

"A job that big and they don't have the money. I asked Sid about it in there and he looked at me like I was crazy. He thought I was asking him about four hundred and fifty dollars."

"Where did he get that amount?"

"That's how much he stole and that's what he thinks all this trouble is about," Clint said. "And I believe him. At least, I believe that's what he believes."

"How could I have been so stupid?" Manuel groaned. "I went after the wrong man, and now he's going to trial for something he hardly even knows about."

"If Judge Warrick is the type of man I think he is, Sid Hogan won't have to worry about a long trial." Before Manuel could get too relieved, Clint added, "There'll be a hanging in no time flat."

For a moment, Clint seriously thought the Mexican was going to be sick. Manuel lost some of the color in his face and clutched one hand to his stomach as though he was genuinely having trouble digesting what Clint had just told him.

"I knew it," Manuel said wearily. "I knew I shouldn't have taken up this line of work. Everything just seemed to fall into place."

"Don't blame yourself, Manuel. You thought exactly what you were supposed to think. Whoever is behind this went through a lot of trouble to leave a trail and several markers that all pointed to Sid Hogan. It's not the first time someone set up a patsy to take their fall for them, but I have to admit they did a pretty good job. They even got the posters changed in their favor."

"I can't let Sid hang for this," Manuel said with steely resolve. "I don't care how much money I was paid, I can't let that happen."

"Sid won't hang. Not for this anyway. He'll have to answer to the crimes he did commit, but not for this one. The man we're looking for is the one who could have shot your partner when he had the chance.

"Any wanted man with a brain in his skull would have killed Susan rather than let you go. He would have killed her and come after you because his life depended on it. That alone tells me a lot, and the rest of my questions will be cleared up real soon."

Manuel nodded at everything that Clint said. "So we're going after this one? You and me."

"No, Manuel. We're not going anywhere. The man we're after will come to us. If my guess is correct, he's here already."

THIRTY-TWO

Clint had been glad to see Susan when he'd run into her on the streets of Sacramento. The truth of the matter was, he was glad to see Manuel, too, even after he knew about the stressful circumstances. He'd enjoyed his time so far in Sacramento because he'd gotten to relax and explore the city without anything too urgent hanging over his head.

He'd enjoyed it at first, anyway.

Maybe he'd just gotten used to being in the middle of a storm and couldn't adjust to life without everything whipping around him. Clint had heard stories like that from men discharged from the Army, especially those that had been in combat. They'd grown accustomed to the action and the risk and living every day as if it were their last. That was why so many men like that turned into lawmen or even outlaws.

It was the way the blood sped through their veins and their hearts hammered within their chests. A man simply didn't get that by becoming a farmer or taking up a quiet life with a quiet family in a quiet town. Some men missed the smell of gunpowder much like a caged animal missed the feel of wide open spaces.

Clint knew that feeling all too well, even as someone who enjoyed the benefits of a quiet, civilized life. Simple pleasures were all well and good, but he couldn't lose himself in them forever. Before too long, Clint had to have a cause worth fighting for or a task that needed doing.

He needed to see new things, talk to new people and see what waited for him in the world at large. He'd felt that need chewing at his belly again very recently. Normally, that would be enough for him to toss the saddle over Eclipse's back and start riding. This time, he'd met up with Susan and Manuel before he'd put Sacramento behind him.

After seeing the petrified look on Sid Hogan's face, Clint knew he'd made the right decision in staying. Judge Warrick had probably already made his mind up about the case before any lawyer said a single word. Clint was no lawyer, so that meant he could only help things one other way.

His way.

And the time to start was now.

Clint felt his blood begin to rush through his veins and his heart beat a little harder in his chest. There was serious business to contend with and some tricky work ahead, but he had to admit he felt good. The storm was kicking up its heels and he was right in the middle of it—right where he was supposed to be.

Of course, those type of things never started out moving too fast. Like a train, they had to build up steam until they were moving along so quickly that nothing could stop them. Clint could feel that they were approaching that point even now. The locomotive had crested over a hill as soon as Manuel and Susan began putting all the various pieces together concerning the way they'd been led around by the nose.

Clint had been there to keep it moving, because the last

thing that should happen was for the train to roll to a stop. After all, that was exactly what the real killer wanted to happen. That had been the purpose of all of this: to divert attention away from himself so he could just walk away from that robbery with all the money and none of the blame.

It was actually a good plan. What it lacked in originality, it made up for in execution. This killer wasn't the first person to think of doing something like this, but he'd sure done a hell of a job.

It was going to be a real pleasure to pull the rug right out from under his feet.

Thinking about that put a smile on Clint's face. The blood was pumping even faster now, and he could feel his heart knocking at the inside of his rib cage. Things were falling into place like timber and rocks forming a dam. The main thing that was in Clint's favor was the fact that he knew the real killer would want to be in town to see Sid Hogan's trial.

After all the trouble he'd gone through to get things this far, the killer simply would have to be present to make sure everything turned out the right way. Sure, it would have been smarter to just push things to a certain point and then leave. But if this train robber was that smart, he wouldn't have been at that house when Manuel and Susan arrived.

He would have been long gone, leaving Sid sitting somewhere waiting for a meeting that would never happen. That's the way Clint would have done it if he'd been in the other man's shoes. Despite the fact that he would never do anything like kill eight people in a train robbery, it helped that he could place himself in the boots of someone who would.

He didn't need to step all the way into that mentality. All he had to do was get far enough into the role so that he could guess what the real killer's next move would be.

The moment he started thinking like the killer, Clint ached to see how well everything had turned out.

Sid Hogan was in a cell and about to plead his case to the deaf ears of Judge Warrick. At this point, there wasn't much of a reason why the real killer shouldn't show up at the hanging and toss Sid a wave right before the platform dropped.

Even Clint had to admit that this killer was fairly smart and very patient. This time, however, patience was anything but a virtue. Whoever this man was, it was doubtful he planned on Manuel and Susan taking a hard enough look at the facts to figure out what they truly meant. Most bounty hunters wouldn't give a damn what the real circumstances were just so long as they got their money.

Manuel had gotten his money, but the circumstances just weren't sitting right in his gut. Susan was a far cry from a typical bounty hunter as well. Even with both of them working together, it had taken one extra factor to start the killer's plan truly unraveling.

That single factor not only saw how everything fit together, but he knew what to do about it. Clint had to admit that he enjoyed being that factor to tear down such a well-executed plan. In the end, he couldn't really blame the killer for not being able to see the end coming. Better men than this one had tried to pull one over on the wrong person.

It was a thief's nature to steal and a killer's nature to kill.

The bad news for this particular killer was that it was Clint's nature to stop him. Even more bad news came in the fact that Clint wasn't alone in this task.

Now that they'd seen their mistake and actually gave a damn about it, Manuel and Susan were willing to help rectify it. Clint had given them each jobs to do, and he had no doubt they were doing them even now. Since Manuel was so proud of his relationship with the U.S. Marshals in the area, he was the one sent out to deal with them.

Susan Connover had her own set of skills, many of which Clint had sampled for himself. Her job was to act as a scout and spy within the city. No matter how hard a thief tried to cover his tracks, he couldn't hide for too long from one specific group: other thieves.

Just as gunfighters enjoyed boasting about their kills to anyone who would listen and spread the word, thieves did plenty of talking on their own. Sure, they weren't as loud as a blowhard in a saloon and didn't talk to as many people, but they talked. And even if the leader of the train robbers was smart enough to keep his mouth shut, there were at least half a dozen others working with him. The smart money would bet that at least one of those others would feel like talking to the right person.

Susan Connover had a special way about her that made men think that she was the right person.

As for Clint, he got to hang back and do every other job that needed doing. Once the man they were after made his big mistake, Clint would be there to mop up.

Always save the best for last.

THIRTY-THREE

Just because Susan didn't like to fight to gain men's attention didn't mean that she didn't know how to do it. While most other women busied themselves by making pretty dresses or saving their pennies to buy them, Susan had always dressed the way she wanted. When everything was said and done, men's clothes were a hell of a lot more comfortable, so those were exactly what she wore.

But underneath the blocky shirts and heavy denim jeans, Susan was all woman. Like every other woman who'd been around her fair share of men, she knew exactly what men wanted and how far they'd go to get at it. Not wanting to go too far in one direction by buying something pink and frilly, she made do with what she had. Fortunately, she had quite a lot.

Before heading over to the saloon district, she unbuttoned the top three buttons on her shirt and pulled the halves open just enough to put on a show, but not enough to look like she'd meant to show anything. Strange as it may have seemed, she found that she always got farther if she let the men think they were getting more than she was willing to give. It was no closely guarded secret among women that they all let men think this way. The plain fact of the matter was that most men just didn't think much farther than the soft, ample curves they could see.

With her shirt kept open just enough to entice and its tails tucked into her jeans to allow her hips to be plainly viewed, Susan made her way from one saloon to another, searching for just the right one. She settled on the Coastal House as her most likely candidate. The place was big enough to have plenty of secluded corners and was seedy enough for those corners to be good and dark.

The moment she stepped into the bar, she could sense that she'd chosen well. Although not a lot of heads turned when she stepped through the door, eyes shifted beneath ridged brows to follow her every move.

She struggled to keep from meeting all of those eyes in turn. It was a fine balance to strike, but Susan quickly hit a confident stride while looking around at only a few of the more obvious gawkers.

Let the rest think they're sneaking their peeks, she thought. *That gives them more chances to do something foolish.*

Walking up to the bar with just the right amount of trepidation creeping into her eyes, Susan leaned with both elbows on the wooden surface so she could cock her hip at an enticing angle. "Isn't there a show in this place?" she asked the bartender.

The man behind the bar looked as though he'd been chewed up and spit out. It was difficult to tell whether the gouges in his face were scars or pockmarks of some kind. One thing was painfully clear about the man. He was ugly. Real ugly.

His lips twisted into something that Susan guessed was a smile. The bartender seemed self-conscious enough to try and hide the chipped, yellow teeth that lined up in his mouth like poorly tended tombstones. "You see a stage in here?"

Susan looked around, more as an excuse to turn at her

waist and stretch her back to the silent delight of the drunks scattered throughout the room. "No. Maybe you should build one."

"You're the best entertainment we had in here for a while, darlin'. You got a name?"

"Sure do," she told him, while smiling as though she enjoyed the slimy excuse for a compliment he'd given her. "But only if I get to hear yours first."

Using one beefy hand to press down a few wayward stalks of greasy hair, the barkeep let his guard down enough to show a few more of his revolting teeth. "I'm Andy."

"Well, hello there, Andy. I'm Susan. Think I can have a drink?"

"That's what I'm here for."

Susan felt a presence closing in on her like the crackle of an approaching storm that tickled the hairs on her arms. She didn't turn to look at the source of that feeling, but concentrated all of her attention on that corner of her field of vision.

"If you make this pretty lady pay for that drink," came a voice from right next to Susan, "you'll have to answer to me."

Susan jumped a bit, as though she'd been startled by the sudden appearance of the man beside her. Turning just a little at the waist and the rest of the way by just using her neck, she made sure not to meet the other man's eyes right away.

"Thank you very much," she said. "My name's Susan."

"I heard."

The man next to Susan was a few inches taller than her and probably only outweighed her by about sixty pounds. He had a bulky frame which strained the seams of his tattered shirt. The gun belt around his waist was worn in and well used. It carried what looked like an Army model .44.

He leaned against the bar, moving his eyes slowly up
and down her body, as if he was drinking in the sight of
her, much the same way he might drink the whiskey inside the glass he held. Once he saw that Susan was getting
uncomfortable, he leaned in and extended his free hand
to her.

"I'm Brandon," he said. "You just get into Sacramento?"

"Actually yes. Does it show?"

"A little. I just know most everybody around here, so
you caught my attention. Of course," he added, dropping
his gaze to the sloping curve of her exposed cleavage,
"that's not the only thing that caught my eye."

Smiling bashfully, but without making an attempt to
cover up, Susan played right into the role that would put
Brandon even more at ease. "I'm passing through here on
my way to San Francisco. Have you ever been there?"

"I've been a lot of places, sweet thing. I sure hope
you're not moving on from here right away."

"Why's that?"

"Because there's plenty of excitement in Sacramento to
curl your toes. I've got stories that you wouldn't believe."

"Mmm," Susan purred. "That sounds exciting." She
dropped her eyes toward the gun at Brandon's side and
pulled in a quick breath. "Have you ever used that gun
before?"

Winking, Brandon replied, "Only if the other fella
doesn't leave me a choice. But I'm sure you don't want
to hear about ugly business like that."

"Don't be so sure." Susan inched closer to him until
her hip brushed up against his. She looked at him and
held her eyes in place, her breath coming in the occasional
gasp. To play up the effect, she imagined the last time
she'd felt Clint's hands on her naked body and his lips
wandering between her legs.

Although Brandon didn't know exactly what was going

through her mind, he sure got the message she was sending. He found his own breath speeding up as well. His skin grew hot on the couple places where her body was touching his own.

"You'd better watch yourself there, darlin'. A man might get the wrong impression."

She smiled and let her eyes wander over his chest much the way his had been studying hers. "And what makes you so sure that's the wrong impression?"

Since time was of the essence, Susan decided to take another couple steps forward. If Brandon had any misgivings about her, he might get suspicious if she moved too fast. But the one thing working in Susan's favor was that Brandon was first and foremost a man.

When she moved her hand up from where it had been resting by her side, Susan let her fingers brush against Brandon's inner thigh. She quickly pulled her hand away, but gave him a warm, slightly embarrassed smile.

"Why don't you come over to my table in the back?" he asked, trying to keep his composure. "I'll tell you some stories."

THIRTY-FOUR

The steam in Manuel's stride died off pretty quickly as soon as he strutted back into the U.S. Marshals' office. Now that the marshals had their prisoner and a contented judge to boot, they didn't much care what the bounty hunter was doing any longer. In fact, when they saw the Mexican come back, they were reminded of all the money they had to hand over, which was more than they'd seen in a long time.

Still, Manuel had a job to do, so he ignored the dirty looks and walked right up to the man in charge. "There's not enough guards on the prisoner," he said.

That was the Mexican's first mistake.

Every marshal in earshot turned to look at Manuel as though the bounty hunter had just walked in off the street and insulted his mother. The tension in the air was thick enough to cut with a knife. From where Manuel was standing, however, he was certainly glad there were no knives laying about.

"What did you just say?" the marshal closest to Manuel asked.

It wasn't that the Mexican was bad with names. He didn't remember the marshal's name because the lawman simply had never given it. Since he could tell that now wasn't the time for formal introductions, Manuel moved right along with what little he already had.

"I suggested that you might want to put some more guards on Sid Hogan."

"No," corrected the marshal. "You said we didn't have enough on him already. We ain't deaf and we ain't incompetent. There's plenty of men guarding that one, so why don't you just run along and spend some of that money we gave you?"

Manuel did his level best to keep his frustration from showing. Clint had asked him to do a simple task and by god, he meant to do it. Of course, the task had seemed a hell of a lot simpler a couple minutes ago.

"Look, amigo. I didn't mean to—"

Manuel was cut off by the marshal's sharply raised hand. Although there were only two other marshals in the room, they closed in around him, making it feel like the place was chock full of angry badges.

"I guess you didn't hear me the first time," the lawman snarled. "You did your job, so make yourself scarce so we can do ours. Talk back one more time and we'll just have to back up that order with a boot to your ass."

Manuel had always had a healthy respect for the law. Mostly, that was because it was usually unhealthy not to respect it. Even though he'd taken up a job that most lawmen didn't much care for, the Mexican still preferred to go along with the men who wore the badges.

It was just good business.

At this point, however, he'd about had his fill of the marshal. By the tone in the lawman's voice and the way he surged forward a bit when he threatened him, Manuel could tell that the marshal was accustomed to other people backing up when he talked that way. Manuel didn't feel like backing up. In fact, his upper body came forward a bit so that he met the lawman nose to nose.

"You hear what I said?" the marshal asked. "Or do I have to say it louder next time?"

"I heard you, señor. And I wouldn't recommend that you shout at me one more time that way."

The marshal took a step back and looked around at the other lawman that was nearby. The second marshal had picked up on the serious tone in Manuel's voice and was stepping forward in the event that his backup was needed.

"You threatening me?" the first marshal asked.

"No. I'm trying to help you, but you would have seen that if you weren't so busy trying to mark your territory like a coyote pissing on a log."

Manuel saw both marshals move their hands toward their holstered guns. Neither one of them went any farther than that, and Manuel knew neither of them had any intention of clearing leather. He wasn't exactly sure how he knew. He just did.

Some folks would call it intuition.

Clint would probably say it was a way of reading someone's eyes.

"There's more of those robbers out there, señor. They'll be coming for this one that you've got in your cell. If I were you, I'd watch him a little closer. That's all I wanted to say."

"You got your money, bounty hunter. Now get the fuck out of my sight."

Manuel held his ground for a moment to take a good look at the marshal. He must have been getting better at reading people's faces, because he saw something that told him his job was done. Without another word, he tipped his hat to both lawmen, turned toward the door and left.

Let the asshole have his victory, Manuel thought.

The marshal kept his eyes glued to the Mexican's back all the way up to the point when Manuel stepped outside and let the door shut behind him. Even then, the lawman let his eyes linger on that spot for a moment just in case that door was going to swing open again.

It didn't swing open. It didn't even budge. Once he heard the Mexican's steps on the boardwalk outside, the marshal let out a single, sniffing laugh. It sounded something like a dog giving one last snuff before admitting he'd lost a scent.

"Can you believe that goddamn son of a bitch," the marshal said to the other lawman, who'd taken up position behind him.

The second marshal shook his head and walked back to his chair. "Damn bounty hunters think they can come in here and call the shots. All of 'em want to wear a badge and are too damn stupid to do it on their own. I had it my way, we wouldn't pay them shit."

"You're right about that." Walking around his desk, the first marshal dropped himself into his own chair and swung his feet up to their regular position on top of his blotter. "Do me a favor, though."

"Yeah?"

"Put some more guards on that prisoner."

THIRTY-FIVE

Clint had chased down enough backstabbers and killers to know how they thought and the patterns they lived by. It wasn't too hard, really. All he had to do was put himself in the frame of mind of a coyote or a vulture. The carrion eaters. Those were the animals most like a man who would make his living by shooting innocent people and picking at the bones.

A vulture on two legs.

Clint smiled at the thought of that. Not only was the notion somewhat amusing, but it was very appropriate. In no time at all he had several ideas running through his head on where the real killer might be and what he would want to do while in town. The only advantage that his target might have was if the killer knew his way around Sacramento better than Clint.

It wasn't much of an advantage, but it might just give the vulture an edge in a sticky situation. That was why Clint had been keeping himself moving since he parted ways with Susan and Manuel. The more of Sacramento he walked, the more he would remember. And the more of Sacramento he committed to memory, the less of an edge that vulture would have.

Whenever he passed locals who looked like they knew where they were going, Clint had to fight back the urge to ask them questions. He didn't need to know much apart from some basic details about the city, but he knew only too well that the smallest thing could boil over into a problem.

He could be recognized by someone who would drop his name at the exact wrong time.

He could ask someone his question, move on and then become the topic of a conversation when the wrong person was listening.

There were plenty of things that could go wrong, and now was the time when something like that would happen. Clint knew he wasn't being paranoid. Just realistic and very careful. Besides that, asking questions and gathering information was someone else's job. If he was going to be part of a team, Clint had to trust that Susan would pull her weight.

As he thought about all of this, Clint's eyes fell upon a shape at the far corner. The shape was a figure in a coat, much like plenty of others wearing similar coats. But as he walked, Clint's eyes stayed on that figure for what felt like a solid couple of minutes.

In reality, it had only been a few seconds, but to him it felt much longer than that. Having learned a long time ago to trust his instincts, Clint figured that he'd spotted something odd about that man in the distance that he just hadn't figured out yet. On some level, his brain was not letting him take his eyes off that man in the coat.

Rather than pull his focus away, Clint lowered his head and turned his body so he wasn't so obvious about where he was looking. He kept his eyes locked on target until the rest of his brain figured out why he felt he had to do so.

Suddenly, in a split second of dim light reflected off a window, Clint had his answer.

The other man had walked in front of a storefront whose window shone a bit of light onto the side of his face. It didn't last much longer than it would take a normal person to blink, but like the flash from a photographer's bulb, that was enough to provide illumination.

Clint smiled to himself and thought about Marcus Kary. Perhaps it was all that chatter on the train about taking photographs that had put that analogy into Clint's mind. If that was the case, Clint owed Marcus a drink because that snap of light in the right direction was enough to show Clint a familiar face.

More specifically, he recognized the other man's face from one of the smaller portraits drawn on the first reward notice Manuel had shown him. Since he'd focused more on the bigger picture at the time, Clint had almost let the rest of those faces slip away. But part of Clint's brain had not only held onto them, it had also picked out the genuine article and stopped Clint in his tracks once the other man had been spotted.

If Clint ever needed a good reason to listen to all of his hunches and follow his gut, this was one of them.

So far, no more than two or three seconds had gone by. It was getting close to the amount of time that would tip off the man in the coat that something was wrong, but not quite. To make sure he didn't push things any further, Clint took his eyes off the other man and bent down to fix the top of his boot.

He watched the vulture circle out of the corner of his eye until the other man turned away and crossed the street. Moving with casual grace that blended in perfectly with the others around him, Clint fell into step with a few pedestrians who just happened to be walking in the right direction. He kept tabs on the man in the coat without once looking directly at him until he'd worked his way up closer and behind him.

Reflexively, Clint looked up to survey his surroundings

as he followed the other man into an alley between a clothing store and a carpenter's shop. Sure enough, it looked as though the vulture was circling toward the rear entrance of a hotel with a decent view of the jailhouse.

There were a few better vantage points in town, which Clint had already scouted out, but this one wasn't quite as obvious and was closer to the Marshals' office to boot. Clint wasn't about to march right into the alley on the other man's heels, so he let the vulture have some slack before moving in to close some of that distance.

If he'd had more time, Clint wouldn't have gone into that alley at all. He would have much rather scouted out the area a bit more and moved in a little later on wherever the man was headed. That sure would have been safer, which meant it would also have been smarter.

But Clint didn't know exactly how much time he had, so he just had to assume that he didn't have much at all. That meant walking into the vultures' nest sooner rather than later, but it didn't mean being stupid as he went about it.

Turning sharply at the last moment, Clint stepped away from the opening to that alley and headed around the block to close in on the hotel from the front. Having sighted his prey and sailed around to get a better angle from which to strike, Clint was reminded of another kind of natural hunter.

The hawk.

THIRTY-SIX

As she talked to Brandon at his own table in the back of the room, Susan had to remind herself that she was the one trying to charm him and not the other way around. It was easy for her to lose sight of her true purpose since the other man appealed to her in so many ways.

He wore his gun like a man who'd used it on more than one occasion and looked out at the world with eyes that were an ice-cold blue that sent chills down her spine. In a way, he reminded her of Clint. He had that same power in his bearing that didn't need any help to show through. It was in his voice whether he was talking or whispering, and it was in his body, especially when he moved in closer to her.

They'd spent a couple hours trading various uncivilized stories, each one trying to top the other while pushing the boundary of what might be considered acceptable. As time wore on, that boundary got pushed back farther as well, just as they moved physically closer and closer.

"So is this really such an exciting place?" Susan asked in one of the few lulls of their conversation.

He finished off the beer he'd been working on and said, "What do you mean?"

145

"I mean it looks like there's a lot of rough types in here, but it doesn't seem like they're doing much apart from drinking. I heard there was some real killers in town."

"And where'd you hear something like that?"

"From someone who'd pay a whole lot of money to meet men like that up close and personal." Susan knew she was taking a risk in steering the conversation so sharply in that direction, but something told her that Brandon wouldn't mind. She'd sized him up as a man who worked for his own interests, although he wasn't about to do just anything for some quick money. This was where she needed to rely on the foundation of attraction and flirting she'd been building this entire time.

Judging by the look in his eye, that foundation of hers was pretty solid. "You're not working for the law, are you?" he asked, his eyes reflecting that he was only partly serious.

Although there wasn't much space left between them, Susan closed it up until her body was resting against his. She slid her hands over his lap, reaching all the way up until she could feel the bulge in his crotch. Smiling when she felt that bulge swell a bit, she said, "I only shared my bed with the law once. It taught me that just because a man carries a gun doesn't mean he knows how to use it."

"Is that a fact, now?"

"Yessir. That's a fact."

"Well there are some men that came into town not too long ago. Actually, it was just the other day. Real killers by the looks of them." Moving his face forward until he could nibble on Susan's neck, Brandon worked his way up until his lips brushed against her earlobe. "They're looking for men to join up with them, and I was thinking about taking them up on their offer. What do you think about that?"

"I think you're just saying that to impress me."

Biting her earlobe a little harder, Brandon tightened his grip on Susan's knee. He felt his blood rush even faster when he realized that she hadn't even tried pulling away from him. "Is that the sort of thing that would impress you?"

Susan let out a quiet, breathy moan which was like thunder in Brandon's ear simply because they were so close together. "Haven't you seen the way I look at you when you tell me about all those things you've done? Oh my god, it gets me hotter than a June bride to think about a man taking charge and running through like a demon with guns blazing."

This was the part that Susan had been working up to. Either Brandon was going to take her at her word and buy into everything she was saying to him or he wouldn't believe a damn thing and would hurt her to salvage his pride. She knew he was the kind of man who enjoyed hurting people, whether that meant robbing them or simply scaring the tar out of them. But he was also a man who lived by his own rules, and Susan didn't think he was so much a killer as a rogue.

The main thing that got him on her side, apart from the way her hand worked between his legs, was the fact that Susan wasn't bluffing. There was a devilish charm to Brandon that made her warm up to him as well as feel a little naughty for enjoying his company so much. Those things combined put a genuine longing in her voice and an urgency in the way she touched him.

"You really do like that, huh?" Brandon asked as his eyes drank in the sight of her squirming before him so brazenly.

"Here," she said, taking his hand and guiding it between her legs. "Feel how much I like it."

She used her thumb to unhitch the top fasteners of her jeans and allowed Brandon to do the rest. His hand was strong in pulling her pants open and slightly down, but gentle when he felt the skin beneath the clothing. He watched as her eyes closed a bit when she felt him moving his fingers through the thatch of hair between her legs. The next thing he felt was the hot, moist lips of her vagina as she writhed slowly in anticipation to feel more.

Suddenly, her eyes snapped open and she took a look around. The rest of the men in the saloon weren't exactly staring at her and Brandon, but they were definitely watching from the corners of their eyes.

"Tell me about these men," she whispered. "Are they rough like you?"

Brandon smirked the way a man did when he knew he'd snuck his way into a woman's favor. "Ain't nobody tougher than me, darlin'."

At any other time, Susan might not have been able to keep herself from laughing at that. Just then, however, it fit. "They're probably just loudmouthed cowboys."

"Not these men. They're train robbers, and they've been spreading the word around here that they need new blood to come with them on their next job."

If she ever needed more proof about her theory that robbers loved to sing their own praises, that was it. Even before she'd taken up as a bounty hunter, Susan knew that about men who lived the dangerous life. The fact of the matter was that she truly loved hearing those stories almost as much as men like Brandon enjoyed telling them.

The excited glimmer in her eye was real and so was the shakiness in her breath when Brandon touched her. She felt something similar to the charge she'd gotten from Clint's hands. They were different, but very much alike as well.

Both men had that aura of danger about them. Clint's was a rare kind of aura that was the combination of him being so confident in his own abilities as well as being the center of so many stories and legends. The air around

Brandon had more of a raw energy to it, like that of a vigorous wolf that hadn't sunk its teeth into many jugulars but was aching to try.

Both men stirred something inside of her, making her wonder now how Brandon would touch her or if he could control himself when she touched him.

Unable to mask the desire she was feeling, Susan asked, "And I guess you want to go with them?"

"I just might."

"Then maybe you could tell me about it."

"I will," Brandon said. "But not here."

"Have you got some place better in mind?"

"I sure do."

"Is it close?"

"Just through that door behind the bar."

She slowly pulled his hands off of her and slid her chair back. "Let's go."

THIRTY-SEVEN

When they got up from their table, Susan felt like she and Brandon were moving at their own speed, independent from the rest of the world. Everyone else in the saloon watched them walk across the room, and they traded a few laughs when Brandon led her into the room behind the bar, but she didn't care.

The only thing on Susan's mind was that she shouldn't be following this man whom she barely knew. She should know better than to lower her guard with a man who freely admitted to being a violent gunhand as well as an aspiring robber. She had a job to do, which she might be able to do well enough just by talking and leading him on.

But the truth was that Susan didn't want to stop after just talking. She wanted to fan the flames that were building inside of her, and nothing fanned them higher than the thought that she was being very, very bad.

The room Brandon took her to was a small storage area with a thick bolt that fit into brackets on either side of the door. It was obvious that the room was also used as a hiding place, since there were rifles propped against the wall and boxes of bullets for everything from pistols to shotguns.

Judging by the way he quickly found the board that fit into the door brackets, Brandon had been in that room before. He even knew where the hook was on the wall for him to hang his gun belt on without having to take his eyes off of Susan. The moment he'd removed his gun, Brandon took her by both hands and roughly pushed her against the wall far from any of the weapons.

"I've got you now," he whispered. "Nobody out there will do a damn thing even if they hear you scream."

"What if I moan?" she asked, pulling open his jeans and feeling inside. "Is it all right if I moan real loud?"

Brandon smiled as though he truly didn't know what to say to that. Just as he thought of something, his breath caught in his throat as Susan's hand closed around the shaft of his erect penis.

He wasn't at a loss for too long, however. As soon as he caught his breath, Brandon began tearing off her clothes just so he could finally get his hands on her naked skin. The moment he got her shirt open, he pushed his hands up under her camisole and cupped her soft, warm breasts.

"Tell me about those killers," she whispered. "Tell me about all the things you'll do after joining up with them."

"They're wanted men," Brandon said, sliding his hands over Susan's plump backside. "And after I join them, I'll probably be wanted, too."

She shifted her weight so that she was standing on the balls of her feet. From there, she moved her hips back and forth, rubbing her damp pussy along the length of his cock. "Will you rob a bank?"

"Maybe even kill a deputy if I have to."

"I want to see you use your gun."

When she saw Brandon start to look over his shoulder, Susan put her fingers beneath his chin and turned his head back to look at her. "Not that one," she said, using her other hand to fit the end of his cock into her pussy. "I want to see how good you use this one."

Brandon's smile grew until it covered his face ear to ear. He grabbed onto her buttocks with both hands, lifted her off her feet and pushed her hard up against the wall. "I'd say my aim's dead on," he told her, just before pushing all the way inside of her.

Spreading her legs open as far as she could, Susan grabbed hold of him with both arms wrapped around his neck and shoulders. She bit down on her lower lip as she took him all the way inside. His hard shaft rubbed against the sensitive skin of her clitoris, sending ripples of pleasure throughout her entire body.

"Oh my god," she groaned.

"You like that?" Brandon whispered, his face held close to her ear as he began pumping in and out of her.

"Harder," she begged.

Brandon was more than willing to comply. He felt her fingers digging into his back and her legs wrap tighter around him. The lips between her legs felt slick and hot wrapped around his penis. When he pulled out of her, she tightened around him as though she didn't want to let him go.

But he had no intention of leaving just yet and pounded into her yet again, slamming her against the wall hard enough to shake some things hanging on nearby hooks or resting on shelves. His rhythm picked up, causing her backside to pound against the wall.

Every time she felt him drive deeply into her, Susan let out a grunting moan. There was no way to compare what they were doing to lovemaking. This was fucking, pure and simple. She'd wanted to feel him inside of her the moment she'd looked at Brandon's face. And now that she was off her feet and had Brandon pumping between her open legs, Susan felt that extra thrill that only came with going into forbidden territory.

Brandon felt that thrill as much, or even more, than she did. He couldn't even see her naked body except for the glimpses he would get when she arched her back and allowed the halves of her shirt to fall away from her breasts. Susan's nipples were erect and her skin was glistening with perspiration even though the only heat in the room came from their bodies.

As he looked down to savor the sight of her abdomen straining in time to his thrusts, Brandon felt her hands grab hold of him even tighter. Her heels dug into him almost enough to cause him some pain, but it soon became clear that she was just trying to climb a little higher on his body. Once her face was level with his, Susan gave him a smile that was dripping with lust.

Using her arms to pull herself up, she began bouncing up and down on his cock, riding him as though he hardly even had a say in the matter. Suddenly, the tables had turned and Brandon was no longer in control of the situation.

Not that he minded it one bit, of course.

In fact, he took a few steps away from the wall so Susan could have more room to lean back and wriggle her hips back and forth as she took him in and out at a quickening pace. She leaned all the way back, until the only thing holding her in place was her hands, which were locked behind his neck, and Brandon's grip, which held onto and caressed the smooth skin of her buttocks. One half of her shirt fell open to reveal one breast and the side of another.

Brandon looked down at her glistening midsection and heaving breasts, wanting nothing more than to press his lips against her skin and taste her flesh. But he couldn't let go and didn't want to break her rhythm, since she was now pumping her hips back and forth, wearing an expression of intense pleasure mixed with near-exhaustion.

She was working hard to ride him, and soon Brandon moved his hips at just the right speed to accommodate her. He could feel his orgasm rushing toward him and had to push her up against the wall again as his knees threatened to buckle. Susan was getting weak as well, and her entire body trembled with the combination of her vigorous exercise and the climax that rolled through her skin like a gust of wind.

Their moves became more powerful, more desperate, more intense as Brandon exploded inside of her. Even as his orgasm started to fade, Brandon didn't want to pull out of her, since the look on her face was total erotic bliss.

Susan clawed at his skin and pumped her hips forward one last time, clenching her pussy around him as her own climax sent pulses of powerful sensation throughout every inch of her body. She opened her eyes, still savoring the feel of Brandon's hard penis between her legs. When she looked at him, she recognized the fact that she could tell him to do damn near anything at all at that moment and he would comply.

That was another thrill she got from dangerous men. In the end, no matter how much blood they'd spilled or how quick they were on the draw, they were still men. And this man, she knew, was hers.

THIRTY-EIGHT

The word was out.

It hadn't taken much to spark some interest in a good number of ambitious gunhands, especially in a place the size of Sacramento. Bigger cities weren't really that different from small towns. As long as there were saloons and gambling, either one would attract the type of men Pete Sanders was looking for.

Pete had been to Sacramento before, so that made his job even easier to accomplish. A few questions asked to the right people was like dropping a lit match onto a field of dry grass. All he had to do was wait for the flames to get to the right places and Pete knew he would have his group of men in no time flat.

What made things even easier was the fact that he didn't even need men that were particularly talented. Like Sid Hogan, all they needed to be was willing to take orders and hold their own in a fight. At least, they had to hold their own for a little while. As long as they stayed alive long enough to catch a bullet or two once the law came after them, that would be fine with Pete. It was just him and two others who'd been with him since the beginning who needed to make their way out of the country.

The law would be after them for only a little while longer. All the marshals needed was a few more bodies to add to their collection and they'd consider the case closed. The bounty hunters would get their money, the judges would get their hangings, and all would be right with the world.

Standing in his hotel room overlooking a healthy chunk of the city, Pete nodded to himself and allowed a smile to work its way onto his face. The one bet that always paid off was doing what nobody else expected. That worked in everything from bedding women to picking which banks to rob. It even worked when outfoxing the law.

It worked amazingly well when dealing with the law.

Pete shook his head and wondered how any man with a brain in his skull could respect a badge. Apart from having a legal means to shoot at another man, the average sheriff or marshal was just a useless bully who couldn't see past the nose on his face.

There were exceptions to that notion, but they were few and far between. In fact, Pete couldn't even think of one right offhand. Perhaps that was because he was staring out his window in the direction of the courthouse.

He wished he could see the jail from his window, but he'd see enough of Sid Hogan's face when it was turning blue at the end of a rope.

That poor bastard.

Thinking about Sid almost made Pete feel sorry for the fool. Almost, but not quite.

Pete's train of thought was interrupted by a sharp knocking on his door. Bracing himself for the light that would invade his dark room, Pete squinted his eyes and glanced over his shoulder.

"What?" he grunted.

"It's me," came a familiar voice from the hall. "I'm coming inside."

Pete nodded to himself without answering the other man. His arms had been folded across his chest, with the left arm covering the right. That hidden right hand was clutching a .32-caliber revolver he'd plucked from its holster the moment he heard that first knock. He lowered the hammer and reholstered the gun only after he saw the face of the man who came in through the door.

"What is it, Jake?" Pete asked.

"It's Sid. He's going to be moved from his cell later tonight."

"What? Why?"

"I think the marshals got wind that we were in town. First, there were more guards posted around the jailhouse, and then I heard about Sid being moved."

"How'd you hear about that?"

"Some of the deputies were talking a little too loud. They strut around like they can walk through fire anyways, so they don't give a shit who else is around when they talk."

"And you didn't hear why they're moving him?"

"No. Maybe it's just what they normally do."

Pete's eyes narrowed as he mulled over what he'd just heard. Something about it just didn't sit too well, although he couldn't quite put his finger on what that was. "When they were talking, did they seem bored? Angry? Restless? What do you think?"

Only just adjusting to the darkness in Pete's room, Jake took a moment to think. "The one who brought the news sounded like he had something stuck in his craw. The one he told was pissed, all right. No question about that."

"Then this is something out of the ordinary. Any other word coming in about the positions that need filling?"

"Plenty. Most of 'em are full of wind, but I recognize one or two that have shot more than their mouth off."

"Good. I want you to select a few of the big talkers and tell them to meet you somewhere near the jailhouse.

Make sure everyone's there in time for the transfer."

"You want me there also?"

"Only to make sure they're in the right place at the right time. I don't care where it is, just be certain they're close enough to get a look at Sid and those marshals when they come out of the jailhouse."

Jake nodded like a soldier receiving his orders. "Should they come heeled?"

"Of course. They might be seeing some action tonight, which might sadly claim their lives. The important thing is that it won't claim ours."

"What kind of action are you talking about? Is Sid not going to make it to his own hanging?"

"Possibly. I haven't decided yet. Just make sure those men are ready to jump when they're supposed to. Be sure you're ready as well."

"Wouldn't it be easier for us to just leave now?" Jake asked. "We could get the money and make it to Canada or Mexico before Sid's trial is over."

"True, but this way we can make sure everything is wrapped up nice and tight. It's the difference between living like kings or living like wanted men. I don't know about you, but I prefer to be a king."

THIRTY-NINE

Clint took his time circling around to the front of the hotel, knowing well enough that he would be able to see if his prey was trying to give him the slip. The trickiest thing about tracking anything, on two legs or four, was knowing what to look for. Once the hunter's eyes were trained properly, it was difficult to get anything past him.

Another thing working in Clint's favor was that there weren't many places for someone to go other than where Clint had already been and where he was going. He didn't much care if the other man made it into the hotel, because he couldn't start too much trouble from within that building.

Once he'd moved around to the front of the hotel, Clint studied the people entering and exiting. Keeping his eyes open and his senses on the alert, he crossed the street and picked a spot that was in the line of sight of anyone who was looking out one of the front windows. From there, he crossed his hands in front of him and looked up at the front of the building.

Knowing that he wouldn't be able to see much through the windows by way of details that mattered, Clint kept his eyes open wide and looked for the subtle signs that

159

he'd spotted a promising possibility. He glanced over the windows that were wide open and lit up for the world to see. Instead, he stared at the windows that were dark, yet still showed signs of movement inside. He paid close attention to the window where he could see a shadowy silhouette standing with just a sliver of his body revealed to the outside.

It seemed obvious to Clint that he'd found the right window. Of course, it was only obvious because he'd been led to this building and knew what he was looking for once he'd gotten there. Without those two important ingredients, the search would have relied solely on blind luck.

Just to make sure he was making his own luck spread as far as it could go, Clint kept his hat low over his face so his eyes were obscured in shadow. He might have been confident that he'd found the right window, but he couldn't be absolutely certain. The way he was playing it, though, all Clint had to be was close.

It took less than a minute for him to realize that he'd been even closer than he might have guessed.

In that short amount of time, the front door of the hotel swung open and another man stepped out. It wasn't the same one he'd followed to get there, but it was one who had the same bearing about him. He wore a gun at his side and carried himself like he knew how to use it. He had cold killer's eyes.

There was only one reason why a dangerous-looking man like that one would be upset over such a simple thing. He must have figured Clint knew what he was looking at and was there to stir up some trouble. That much was plainly displayed on the armed man's mouth, which was drawn into a straight, angry line. It was even easier to see in his slitted, piercing eyes.

But those slitted eyes didn't have a chance to fix on what they were after. By the time the armed man had stepped out of the hotel, Clint was out of sight and watching from the shadows of a nearby alley. He held his hat in one hand to change the shape of his outline, just in case the armed man could glimpse it in the dark opening where Clint stood.

The armed man took another couple of steps outside, glanced around and then did the one thing that Clint had been waiting for. He looked up to that window with the silhouette and shrugged his shoulders.

That one gesture not only confirmed what Clint had suspected, but also told him where the group's leader was staying. It was more than any hunter could ask for at that stage of the game. The next thing on Clint's agenda was to check in on Susan and Manuel to see if their luck had been as good as his own.

On the other hand, he almost didn't see how it could have been.

"Well?" Pete said once the third man entered his room. "Did you find him?"

The third man's name was Cory Tillman. Although the last name sounded similar to that of Bill Tilghman, there was no relation whatsoever to the more well-known figure. Of course, that never stopped Cory from benefiting from those who didn't know any better.

Cory had been riding with the other two for enough years to know what Pete's reaction would be the moment he opened his mouth.

"I couldn't find anyone out there," Cory said. "Nobody that looked like the one you were talking about."

"Well, he was there," Pete said, his anger growing and tainting his voice with a scratchy snarl. "I saw him walk right across that street and look up here like he knew I was standing here. He was tall, wore a coat and had a look about him that I didn't much care for."

"I'll bet he's the same one that followed me here," Jake

said. "He got a look at my face and started dogging my tail. I thought I lost him before I got here, but I guess he made it here after all."

"Yeah," Pete said softly as he turned once again to look out the window. "I guess he did at that."

"You sure you didn't see him anywhere?" Jake asked.

Cory nodded sharply. "There wasn't anyone out there like that, but I can check the area. Hell, it's my ass on the line here, too."

"You're goddamn right it is," Pete snarled. "It's all of our asses if this doesn't come off properly."

Having already turned his back on the other two so he could open the door, Cory was just stepping into the hall when he said, "I knew we shouldn't have come here."

Pete spun around on the balls of his feet and sped across the room like a cat pouncing on a cockroach. For as fast as he moved, he barely made a sound as he breezed past Jake so he could reach out and grab hold of Cory by both shoulders.

With one gesture, Pete dragged Cory back inside and tossed him all the way across the room, until the other man's back slammed against the wall next to the window. Before Cory even had enough time for anger to replace the shock in his system, Pete's gun was drawn and its barrel was digging underneath Cory's chin.

"Tell me what you said again," Pete ordered as he pushed the gun up a little harder into Cory's jaw. "I don't think I heard you the first time."

Cory's face reflected plenty of things. There was anger and surprise, but not one bit of fear. "You heard me right, Pete. I don't think we should be here at all. We were lucky enough to get Sid in that jail cell instead of any of us, but he'll tell everything about us the moment he gets his day in front of a judge."

"Maybe he will. Maybe it won't matter what he says."

"Look here, now. We came here to make sure the law

thought they had their man once Sid was brought in, and it looks like that's the case. The bounty hunters are paid off, the marshals are content to sit on their asses, and there's no more posses coming after us. Hell, there isn't even another reward posted for the rest of us. We got what we came for. It's time to leave."

Slowly, Pete lowered his pistol, until he finally dropped it back into his holster. "You're right." He looked over to Jake and said, "I know you're probably thinking the same thing and you're both right. We got what we came for. Just make sure you get those locals on the street during that transfer, and after tonight, we'll be Canadians."

FORTY

Clint checked his watch one more time. Rather than put the timepiece back into his pocket, he kept it in his hand, since he knew he'd be checking it plenty more times until Susan and Manuel showed up for their prearranged meeting. Although neither of the other two were late just yet, Clint was getting anxious, which didn't make the minutes seem to flow by any quicker.

Just as he was about to flip open his watch one more time, Clint heard something approaching the shadowy corner where all three of them had agreed to meet. Clint didn't move more than a few muscles, but his entire body was ready for the worst as he shifted his gaze to look at who was approaching his spot.

The figure looked vaguely familiar, but not enough to put Clint at ease. It wasn't until Manuel lifted his chin enough for his face to be seen that Clint relaxed the hand that had been drifting toward his gun.

"There are plenty of good saloons in town, amigo," the Mexican said as he walked up to stand next to Clint. "Even the bad ones would be better than meeting on a dark street in the cold."

"Cold? You've been spending too much time away

from the real cold, Manuel. Has your new business made you soft?"

"Not as much as the business you've put me in. I swear these marshals want to kill me themselves, and having me pester them all night long isn't helping matters. This could cost me money, you know."

Clint waved off the other man's griping as though he was swatting a fly. "Get used to it. Bounty hunters aren't the law's favorite people, and that goes for just about any jurisdiction. Did you get everything done?"

"*Sí.* After they put some more guards at the jailhouse, I came back and asked them to do what you said."

"And?"

"They must have seen some of the *cabrones* you were looking for, because it just took a little push to get them to consider moving Sid to another place." Manuel clapped his hands together and rubbed them as a brisk wind tore down the street. "That marshal in charge acted like it was his idea."

"You know when it's going to happen?"

"Midnight. That's what I heard before I left, anyway. Tell me something, amigo. How did you know you could arrange for any of this to happen?"

"I didn't," Clint answered with a smirk. "If the marshals didn't agree to move Sid, I would have settled for putting word out that it was going to happen anyway."

"That's awful quick to spread a rumor, amigo. I didn't know you were such a talkative man."

"Actually, it's not my specialty," Clint said as he turned to look at someone walking toward them both. "But there is someone who's built for the job."

"Built for what job?" Susan asked as she stepped up next to Clint. "And watch how you answer me, Clint Adams, because the wrong thing could just get you hurt."

"I was talking about spreading valuable information and making sure it gets to the wrong ears. Manuel here didn't think you could do it in such a short amount of time."

"What?" Susan said, leaning over and smacking the Mexican on his arm. "I'll have you know I did one hell of a good job. I even got close to someone who knows firsthand about a certain murderous robber who's looking for some hired guns and needs them right quick."

Manuel looked over to Susan with a bit of a scowl. "How close did you get, Connover?"

Smiling in a way that Clint definitely recognized, she shifted on her feet and said, "Pretty close."

Manuel rolled his eyes. *"Ay caramba."*

"All right," Clint said. "Without getting into too much of the nitty-gritty, I'll assume you got your job done."

"His name is Brandon Merrick," she reported. "Ever hear of him?"

Both Manuel and Clint shook their heads.

"Well, that doesn't surprise me too much. I got him to talk some more after we . . . well . . . just after. Anyway, he was going to meet up with someone at the Coastal House saloon after I left, but I stuck around for a bit longer and got a look at the one he was supposed to meet."

Manuel's eyes lit up as though he could already smell another reward headed his way. "You saw him?"

When she looked back at the Mexican, Susan had that same hungry look in her eyes. "It was Jake Hucksley." To Clint, she said, "Jake's been running with Pete Sanders ever since the beginning. He's even on that first wanted poster we showed you."

"I think I got a look at him myself," Clint said. He went on to describe how he'd followed that familiar face to a nearby hotel and the encounter that followed once he got another of the group to come outside.

"That one sounds like Cory Tillman," Manuel said. "And he's not related to Bill."

"I didn't think he was," Clint answered.

Susan seemed to be getting impatient and quickly got the other two's attention. "Anyway, like I was saying, Brandon met with Jake at the Coastal House and found out that him and some of the others are going to meet up at midnight."

"What others?" Clint asked.

"The others that want to join up with Jake, Pete, and Cory. They're supposed to meet in front of a steakhouse called Mil's."

Nodding, Clint said, "I know the place. I've eaten there a few times over the last couple days. It's not too far from the courthouse. I think I know why they're meeting there."

"The transfer?" Manuel asked.

To that, Clint only had to nod.

"Are you sure about all of this?" Manuel asked Susan.

She nodded with absolute certainty. "He didn't mind talking after we . . . well . . ."

"Just after," Clint finished.

"Yeah."

"Don't be too jealous, amigo. Connover here has a problem with giving men with guns everything they want."

She laughed and smacked the Mexican's shoulder again in the same spot. "The only problem you have is that I haven't given you a taste. I think you're the jealous one."

"Maybe I am. Why is it that—?"

"You two can finish this over a drink," Clint said. "First round's on me." He flipped a silver dollar into the air toward both bounty hunters just to see which one would go after it first. Manuel was probably too frustrated by Susan's teasing and reached up for the coin after she'd already snatched it from the air.

"You're not coming?" Manuel asked.

Susan dropped the coin into her pocket and said, "I

hope you're not jealous, too, Clint. I was hoping we could get together later and have a drink by ourselves."

"You two did a great job," Clint said. "And I really admire the fact that you're going through so much trouble to clear this up even after you've already gotten your money."

"Money isn't everything, amigo."

"That's right. And that's why I want you two to have your drink somewhere far from Mil's. There's still some work to be done, but it's the kind of thing more suited to me, and me alone. Having all three of us around would just draw too much attention."

"And what about our drink?" Susan asked.

"I'm looking forward to it, but . . ."

She smiled and nodded. "After."

FORTY-ONE

Sid Hogan was escorted down the street by a formation of U.S. Marshals that looked like a funeral procession. The lawmen matched their pace to Hogan, who was shackled at the wrists and ankles, slowing the entire group to a snail's pace. Although Sacramento was far from quiet even at that late hour, the local law had come through earlier to make sure there were as few people along the marshals' path as possible.

On the surface, it seemed that the area had been cleared pretty well. Of course, that part of town wasn't usually too busy after dinnertime anyway, since most of the saloons and night spots were located elsewhere. But the marshals were in a hurry and only a few of them were truly convinced there was a threat anyway.

The remaining lawmen thought that the ones who did believe were either jumping at shadows or trying to make it seem as though they were doing something else besides acting as nanny to the prisoner who had been dumped into their laps. There were five marshals on the street in all, as well as a few local deputies who stood by on the boardwalk here and there to act as more casual escorts.

As they filed by, the marshals tipped their hats to the deputies and shuffled along.

"What the hell are they doing here?" one of the marshals asked the man walking next to him.

The other marshal glanced back at the deputy they'd just passed, who was the only local lawman still in sight. "Probably trying to feel like he's got something important to do."

None of the other marshals commented on that, since they didn't have anything nice to say.

In the middle of the small group, Sid Hogan struggled to walk as quickly as he could while hefting the length of chains along with him. The look on his face was anxious and fearful. All he knew was that he'd been dragged out of his cell, shackled and pushed down the street without a single word for an explanation. After being treated like a dog on a leash by bounty hunters and lawmen alike, Sid was getting used to keeping his mouth shut and just letting things happen to him.

The procession kept right on moving, wending its way to the courthouse and the set of prison cells within. Those cells were used to hold prisoners during their trial and were in the cellar of the building itself, which made them somewhat more secure. Also, that was the only other place that the marshals could think of putting Sid since it seemed that the jailhouse wasn't as secure as they'd thought.

The marshal in charge of the operation walked at the head of the line. Beside him was the man who'd been assigned to this area for almost as long as his superior.

"You really think this is necessary?" the second marshal asked.

The lawman at the front of the group shrugged and replied, "I didn't much like the look of the fellas I saw watching the jailhouse."

"But that could be anything. Is it worth all of this?"

"Maybe, maybe not. All I know is that Judge Warrick is trying this one's case, and I'd rather take a walk tonight just to be careful than do anything that would put me on Warrick's bad side."

The second marshal nodded and smiled, more out of discomfort than humor. "You got a point there. Besides that, if Warrick's trying him, this poor bastard probably won't be around much longer to trouble us anyway."

Everyone in the procession got a good laugh out of that comment.

Everyone, that is, except for Sid Hogan.

FORTY-TWO

Pete didn't know what the building was that he'd broken into. The only thing that mattered was that it was two floors tall and positioned in the right place along the way he figured the marshals would be walking with their prisoner. He'd approached from the back of the building, broke open the rear door and found his way to the stairs that led to the upper floor.

By the looks of it, the place was some kind of clothing store. It was dark and empty and fit every one of Pete's other criteria, so that was all that mattered. The stairs were narrow and especially treacherous in the dark, but he managed to climb up them without too much difficulty. As he moved, he didn't even feel like he was in charge of his motions.

Pete's muscles seemed to move on their own, like a group that had already been given their orders. What concerned Pete more was that he keep quiet and get his job done. As he climbed the stairs, he was already thinking ahead to where to position himself in the building. As he walked around the few rooms on the top floor, he was already thinking about looking out through a window as opposed to climbing up to the roof. And when he finally did make his way out onto the roof, he was already planning his escape route.

All of this happened in less time than he'd planned. Kneeling down with only a sliver of his right side peeking out from behind the store's sign, Pete lifted the hunting rifle to his shoulder and busied his hands with checking over the weapon one last time.

From where he was situated, Pete could see the marshals rounding the corner and making their way toward the shop. He could also see the other men huddled in a few scattered alleys nearby. Jake and Cory were there as well, but the shadows were too thick for Pete to see their faces. He just had to figure they would do their parts and get the hell out of there.

If they didn't, they probably wouldn't make it out of Sacramento alive.

Pete thought about that without a flicker of emotion as he levered a round into the rifle's chamber, raised the weapon to his shoulder and sighted on the head of the closest marshal.

"All right," Jake whispered to the anxious new faces gathered around him. "Sid's our partner and we need him to pull off that bank job I was telling you all about. There's only five or six marshals guarding him, so this should be easy." Jake kept his voice strained and his words coming at a quick pace so the other men around him didn't get a chance to think. He'd already fed their greedy imaginations with promises of cashing in on some make-believe bank job of which Sid Hogan was the mastermind.

Judging by the intense, slightly overwhelmed look in all the new men's eyes, all of Jake's efforts had come together nicely. There were eight hopeful recruits in all. Five of the men were in the alley with Jake and the other three were nearby getting a similar inspirational speech from Cory.

One or two of the men looked like they were about to question what they were set to do, but it was too late. The marshals rounded the corner, and Jake stabbed his finger toward them while drawing his pistol with his other hand.

"There they are," Jake said, loudly enough to be heard by every single one of the lawmen and robbers alike. "Take 'em down!"

Jake punctuated his command by shoving the closest new recruit out of the alley and firing a shot at the marshals. Like any other battlefield, all questions flew out of the participants' minds the moment the first shot was fired. Across the street, there was a similar explosion of fire and motion as Cory got his group to move as well.

All of the men in the alley with Jake let out a holler and charged from the shadows with guns blazing. Jake was right there with them until the others had all run past him. Although he kept firing toward the procession, Jake hung back and moved toward the cover of darkness.

The fire had been lit. There was no need to stand in the middle of the flames.

The marshals might have been caught flat-footed, but they were far from easy prey. After all, Sid Hogan could have walked himself to the courthouse if nobody thought there was going to be any trouble. The only thing that took some of the lawmen back was that the men they'd thought were simply paranoid had actually turned out to be right.

As soon as the first gunshot cracked through the air, all of the lawmen had their guns ready and were searching for the source of the shot. That first bullet whipped through the air above the procession, causing Sid to drop to the ground and cover his head with both hands.

There were two marshals close to Jake's alley and both of them were already aiming toward the dark opening when the armed men began streaming out. Both of the lawmen squeezed their triggers, and since there were less than a dozen yards separating them from their targets, the two of them tied in drawing first blood.

One of Jake's men spun around on one heel as a bullet tore through his left forearm. The man next to him wasn't so lucky and caught a piece of hot lead square in the chest. The impact knocked him back like he'd been kicked by a mule, sending him straight into the man behind him. Air sucked in through the gaping hole in his chest and his eyes glazed over with a mixture of shock and sorrow. He was dead before his back hit the dirt.

For the most part, the men who'd met Jake and Cory that night were small-timers looking to make a name for themselves. They all had their reasons for wanting to live outside the law, but none of those mattered to the men who were supposedly going to hire them. Those reasons didn't even matter to the recruits themselves once the lead started to fly.

In less than a second, everyone who had a gun was pulling the trigger. Blood was flying through the air soon after the lead found its mark. To Jake, Cory, and Pete the sight was glorious.

FORTY-THREE

"Come on," Pete whispered as he sighted down the barrel of his rifle. "Just stick your head up for me."

He was waiting for a clear shot at Sid Hogan's head. With all the shots being fired and all the confusion that had been spread, there wasn't going to be a better time to make sure the prisoner didn't talk. Once that was done, he could pick off the rest of the recruits to give the law a nicely wrapped bundle and make them think they'd done their job.

When he saw Hogan start to get up and look for a better place to hide, Pete grinned and took a deep breath. His finger tightened around his trigger and froze the moment he heard heavy footsteps come from directly behind him.

"It's all over," came a voice from the darkness. "Put the rifle down."

Pete almost had his shot. He entertained the thought of taking it and dealing with whoever was behind him, but held off. Killing Sid wouldn't do a damn bit of good if Pete allowed himself to die on that rooftop. Figuring the fight had a ways to go before it ended, Pete lowered the rifle from his shoulder and turned to look behind him.

Clint was there waiting for him, holding the Colt at hip level.

Recognizing the deadly efficiency in Clint's eyes, Pete stood so he could face him. He still hadn't let the rifle drop from his hands.

"There's a lot of money waiting for me after this," Pete said.

Clint watched Pete closely, preparing himself for anything. "Let me guess. There's about twenty-seven thousand dollars waiting for you."

Nodding, Pete added, "You can earn a cut of it by letting me finish what I've started. The shooting's already begun. It's too late to do anything about that now."

"I got a look at those men that you tossed into the mix. They're cannon fodder. Not a one of them is a match for those marshals. Even combined, they're outmatched. If they're willing to shoot at U.S. Marshals, those men are going to get what they deserve."

"But you must know there's more going on here than just that fight down there."

"Sure I do," Clint said. "But you're the key. Without you, Sid lives and talks about you and the rest of your men who are hiding down there waiting for you to make your move. You don't make your move, and none of the rest goes off, either. Sound like I got it right?"

Pete didn't say a word to that, which was more than enough to answer Clint's question.

"You think you got this all figured out?" Pete asked.

"Not all, but enough. You can explain the rest at your trial, or you can take it to your grave. Either way, you won't be picking off anyone with that rifle of yours."

Letting out a breath, Pete lowered his hands so that his rifle was hanging down by his waist. His shoulders slumped and he dropped his chin down in defeat. "What can I say? Looks like you got me over a barrel. Here, take the rifle." With that, Pete snapped his arms back and forward again so he could pitch the rifle straight into Clint's face.

Clint squeezed off a shot, but his aim was thrown off by the rifle, which hurtled toward him and smashed into his chest and chin. When he'd batted away the rifle, Clint paused before taking another shot because his target had moved.

Crouching low, Pete darted to one side and rolled to Clint's left. When he came to a stop, he had his pistol drawn and was ready to return fire.

"What the hell do we do now?" Susan asked, ducking behind a water trough as several shots whipped past her head.

Manuel was right beside her, clenching his teeth as the gunfire exploded around him on all sides. "We chip away at these *cabrones* as much as we can because Clint is somewhere in the middle of this."

After taking a deep breath, Susan nodded once and lifted her pistol. "Sounds like a plan to me. At least some of these guys have to be worth something, right?"

"I never thought about that!"

Once they'd picked the path they were going to ride, Susan and Manuel stood up and ran for the trough that was closer to the raging gunfight. They announced their presence by firing their guns as they ran, each one of them dropping one of the ambushers with the first couple of shots.

Clint didn't even feel the impact of the rifle that had been thrown at him. What hurt more was the fact that he'd lost his aim for that crucial split second. He didn't bother trying to line up another shot right away because he knew Pete would be quick to follow up the distraction he'd created.

Sure enough, Clint felt a solid impact in his side followed by a stabbing pain when he tried to pull in a breath. Although he didn't hear the shot, Clint saw the flash of sparks followed by the gout of smoke after the bullet had torn across his ribs. The pain was only temporary, however, and Clint forced it to the back of his mind.

The rooftop wasn't that big an open space, but there was as much area as the parlor of a medium-sized house. That space seemed even smaller to Clint, who was in the middle of it with no cover and another man taking shots at him. Pete had been rushing for that first shot and still managed to graze him. Clint knew he would be dead in a matter of seconds if he took the time to turn and get a clear look at the other man.

Since there wasn't anything to hide behind on the roof, Clint moved in the direction that gave him the most room to maneuver. He had to be careful, however, since that direction led straight off the side of the building.

Clint didn't allow himself to think about falling off the edge and just threw himself forward as if he'd sprouted wings. With both arms extended, Clint pushed off with his legs as Pete fired round after round in his direction.

Lead hissed through the air, but was inches behind Clint as he landed with his chin tucked against his chest and his body angling downward into a somersault. Following his gut rather than his eyes, Clint shot one leg out to stop his momentum and used the other to twist himself around so that he was facing the spot where Pete was standing.

His muscles ached from being twisted at such an odd angle, and his ears rang with the last shot that was fired at him. The only thing on Clint's mind, however, was aiming his next shot, because he knew he wouldn't get a chance to follow it up.

His eyes strained through the gunsmoke to find Pete crouching in the darkness. Actually, he could only make out a vague outline, but that was enough to guide his hand as he brought up the modified Colt and squeezed the trigger.

Pete dropped to one leg, struggled to maintain his focus, but quickly dropped over to land on his side.

Clint stayed down for a bit as well, until he was sure the other man wasn't about to get up. Only then did Clint get back onto his feet and walk over to where Pete was laying.

"You . . . you're throwing away a fortune," Pete snarled through a mouthful of spit-up blood.

"That's the story of my life," Clint answered. "Now get up. You've got an appointment with Judge Warrick to keep."

Clint's bullet had drilled a nasty hole through Pete's left leg, but it wasn't anything too serious. After a bit of struggling and muttered curses, Pete did manage to stand up and face Clint. The men stared at each other for a few moments, and Pete began taking steps backward, until he'd gone as far as he could go.

Recognizing the fatal look in Pete's eyes, Clint squared his shoulders and warned, "Don't be stupid."

Pete thought about Clint's words for a couple seconds, weighed his options and made his decision. His gun had snapped upward and his finger tightened on his trigger. The hammer rose over Pete's final bullet, but Clint's hand had snapped up even quicker and the Colt barked one more time.

The round caught Pete in the forehead, creating a third eye that stayed wide open as his body spun around and dropped off the side of the building.

Clint walked over to the side and looked down at where the corpse had landed. Just then, Manuel's words drifted through his mind.

"It's a long way down," Clint said quietly to the dead man below. "A long way down indeed."

FORTY-FOUR

The U.S. Marshals had taken a few hits, and one of their number was down, but none of the lawmen would be put in the ground anytime soon. They'd reacted quickly enough to the initial assault to have gotten things well in hand before too much time had passed by.

Three of the lawmen had each dropped to one knee and calmly picked off the oncoming attackers one by one. After some of their own had been killed, the rest of the robbers lost their steam and began throwing down their weapons and running, or simply giving up where they stood. In all, five of the recruits would be put in the ground thanks to the botched raid.

Having watched the entire scene from afar, Jake and Cory were about to make a quiet exit when they spotted Manuel and Susan entering the fray. By the time the bounty hunters had made up their minds to throw in with the marshals, the fight was almost over.

"Over there," the head marshal had said while pointing to the alleys where Jake and Cory were standing. "They came from there. Clean out the rest."

Susan was fast enough to chase down Cory, but Manuel wasn't quite so quick on his feet. No matter how fast

Jake was, though, he wasn't fast enough to outrun the bullet from Manuel's pistol. The Mexican was dragging the unconscious train robber into the street with the others when he saw Pete topple from the nearby rooftop. Soon after, Clint was stepping out of that same building.

"You missed all the fun, amigo," Manuel said to Clint.

"I could see quite a bit from where I was. Besides, I thought I asked you two to sit this one out."

"You did. I just didn't listen."

"Well, thanks for the backup, Manuel. I owe you two another round of drinks."

"I don't think you really needed the backup, but I'll take the drinks. Perhaps next time our paths cross?"

"I was thinking more of tonight. Or," Clint added with a shrug, "maybe tomorrow or sometime over the next couple weeks."

"Couple weeks?"

"For the trial," Clint said, dropping his arm over Manuel's shoulder. "We're witnesses to who's really behind that train robbery and need to tell our story to Judge Warrick. It's either that, or let Sid there hang anyway, and I went through too much to let that pan out that way."

"But Sid is a robber, too," Manuel said. "He's no innocent bystander."

"True, but he didn't kill eight innocent people on that train. He'll stand trial for his robbery, but that's not exactly Judge Warrick's jurisdiction. I have a feeling he won't mind cooling his heels in prison instead of dying at the end of a rope."

The Mexican grudgingly nodded his head and walked back to the marshals. Since Jake and Cory were still alive and kicking, he thought Sid had a real good chance of getting out of his bind. Those chances only increased when Clint Adams stepped forward as one of three witnesses speaking on Sid's behalf.

For all he'd been through, Clint didn't look worn out

at all. In fact, he looked more energetic than when the night had started. That might have been because of how things had turned out, but that was only a partial reason. A much bigger reason for his high spirits was rushing toward him with arms wide open, hair flowing behind her and a big smile on her face.

Susan ran into Clint's arms and wrapped her legs around him as he swept her off her feet.

"Who were you talking to back there?" Clint asked.

"What do you mean?"

"I saw you talking to one of those gunmen that the marshals were taking into custody. It looked like you two knew each other."

"Oh, he's just some man that I met. I had to tell him good-bye before he was taken away."

Watch for

THE RED QUEEN

266th novel in the exciting GUNSMITH series
from Jove

Coming in February!

J. R. ROBERTS
THE
GUNSMITH

JAKE LOGAN
TODAY'S HOTTEST ACTION WESTERN!

MEET THE OLD WEST'S REAL-LIFE
"GOOD GUYS"

WHITE HATS

EDITED BY
ROBERT J. RANDISI

BUFFALO BILL CODY, BAT MASTERSON,
AND OTHER LEGENDARY HEROIC FIGURES OF
AMERICA'S OLD WEST GET THE ROYAL
TREATMENT IN 16 STORIES FROM ESTEEMED
WESTERN AUTHORS.

0-425-18426-9

AVAILABLE WHEREVER BOOKS ARE SOLD
OR
TO ORDER CALL 1-800-788-6262